THE
TOPAZ BROOCH

SALLY PALMER
THOMASON

COLD RIVER STUDIO
NASHVILLE, TENNESSEE

Published by Cold River Studio, Nashville, Tennessee

www.coldriverstudio.com

First Edition: 2012

Printed in the United States of America
ISBN 978-0-9848044-7-4

for my family

Author's Note: *For the readers' ease, I chose not to use* thee *and* thou, *the seventeenth century Quakers' form of address both in speech and writing, or the Quakers' established numerical designation for months and days of the week. However, I have used* First Day *instead of Sunday to emphasize the importance of the day that the Quakers set aside for worship.*

Until the mid-seventeenth century surnames were not used by native Welshmen; a son's given name was tied to his father's name for only one generation. For example, when a man named Thomas had a son named John, the son's name would be John ap (of) Thomas. John's father's name would be tied to his father's given name, for example Thomas ap Rufus.

INTRODUCTION

T he oval topaz, no bigger than a quarter, is surrounded
by tiny dark grey seed pearls and backed by a smooth
slice of hammered gold. As I gaze into its luminescent
clarity, I wish that my genes carried some of the clairvoyant
fire of Rumanian gypsies or Egyptian soothsayers rather than
so much of the pragmatic, practical stuff of Presbyterian Scots
and German mathematicians. I long to conjure out of this
lovely chip of crystalline wonder stories of love, loss, intrigue,
joy, hope, adventure, boredom: tales of life gathered from the
minds and hearts of my female ancestors who have worn this
jewel since the last decade of the seventeenth century.

The delicate setting, minute oyster pellets encircling the
forsythia-colored gem, is probably original. However, in the
seventy years that I have known the piece, its presentation has
varied from brooch to dinner ring, pendant, and lavaliere.
Perhaps at some point, in keeping up with style, it was a
watch fob or bauble on a fashionable bonnet, but the life of
this precious stone reaches far beyond the brief time-flutter

of family possession. Eons before my traceable lineage came into being, its beginnings were probably cradled in a crevice of craggy granite, deep in the mountains of central Eurasia, caught in the formation of emerging continents traversed by animals and people who left no written record of existence.

As to the known history of the brooch, family legend holds that it heralds a most heroic beginning and was passed down mother to daughter, or daughter-in-law, for over three hundred years. But, like information whispered from one ear to another in the child's game of gossip, the story that accompanies the piece was most likely stretched or compressed by the whim of the teller, misremembered or forgotten through the passage of time. The story my mother told when she lovingly presented me with the family heirloom on the eve of my wedding as "something old" for good luck does not quite square with family records I uncovered through genealogical research in later years. However, although she placed the country of origin as Ireland rather than Wales (my mother loved to trade on her Irish heritage), both lands within the British realm hold Celtic roots. And more importantly, the essence of the tale, even though the location was slightly skewed, squares with historical facts.

Historical research can tell us much about the activities, political convictions, and faith of our fathers. However, the dreams, doubts, disappointments, and personal triumphs of their daughters and wives—the lives and secrets of ordinary women—are largely lost behind the veil of yesteryears.

I long for my topaz treasure to be a crystal ball, not to foretell the future, but to reveal its past. Yet, no matter how hard I strain to see through and beyond the facets of this sparkling yellow gem, no images appear. The antique charm twinkles forth in sphinx-like splendor, leaving those of us who wear its luster to fill in the links with imagination and intuition.

In telling this story I have built on a slender thread of family myth, amplified by genealogical research and readings from history and literature to create context for the first two women in my family who wore the topaz brooch. All of the main characters in the story of the Topaz Brooch are my ancestors. The dates and locations of their births and deaths have been verified. However, their characters, personalities, activities, the actual events of their lives, are a product of my imagination.

*I cannot cause light. The most I can do
is to put myself in the path of its beam.*
—Annie Dillard

PART ONE

LYDIA

CHAPTER ONE

The cross and magic co-habitated Wales for many centuries...
—Jan Morris, *The Matter of Wales*

April 30ᵗʰ 1677

Brambles scratched at her hands, low hanging branches slowed her pace, and Lydia worried whether this was the right path, or indeed a path at all. When she left home, the meadow grass around her house sparkled with dancing sun motes, and the fresh April air, bursting with new life, smelled green. But now in the dense woods of giant rowans, oaks, and prickly hawthorn, it was like a dank, dark cavern. She felt, but could not see, hundreds of curious eyes watching her every step. Stopping to retie the dark indigo sunbonnet covering her mass of chestnut curls, Lydia wondered if she was lost. Maryd said that the path would be narrow and difficult to follow, until she came to the bog, but this trail was little more than a badger track. What a horrible place to loose one's way. Should she turn back? No one else in the family had been awake when she snuck out of the house at the cock's first crow. Unwilling to take the time to get properly dressed, she had hurriedly pulled on her long homespun shift, not bothering with the heavy house apron her mother insisted she wear now that she was no longer a child. No one except Maryd would have a clue as to where she might be, and Maryd's sense of direction was terrible. Yet, Maryd's sister's tale was intriguing.

Yesterday when Lydia told Maryd about her dream, her friend had listened intently, wrinkled her freckled brow, then pulled Lydia down to sit beside her. Maryd's father was a cottager on Lydia's father's farm, and the girls, both in their fifteenth year, had always known each other, always been best friends. Sitting on the huge flat rock at the edge of the meadow between their two houses, a favorite meeting place for sharing secrets and dreams, Maryd had shaken her head slowly, her two blond pigtails swaying back and forth like pendulums. Lydia had never seen her friend so serious as she pronounced in a low, even voice, "You must go to Mabonig. He could tell you what it means."

"Mabonig? Who is Mabonig?"

"Honestly, Lydia, you have never heard of Mabonig? Why, he is the old man who lives in the woods. He talks to the Little People."

"Talks to the Little People?" Lydia sat up straight and leaned closer to her friend. "Is he a wizard?"

"I think so. People say he spends part of his time with our people and lives the other half of his life in the Other-world."

"Really?" Ever since Lydia was a little girl, she had heard tales of such folk, but had never talked to anyone who actually had seen a Little Person, let alone anyone who had been to the Otherworld. "Do you know anyone who has talked to him?"

Maryd's pale blue eyes danced. "Well, Bridget said I was never supposed to tell anyone, but I don't really think she would mind my telling you, if you promise, cross your heart, not to breathe a word to anyone else." Looking sternly at Lydia, Maryd lowered her voice, "She's afraid that the Little People might get angry, do something bad to one of the twins. Maybe both."

"Maryd, what ever are you talking about? You've got to tell me now. I promise never to tell a soul."

"Well, three summers past, my sister Bridget visited Mabonig when she was pregnant. He warned her that the Little People might try to steal one of her twins when they were born and advised her to take special precautions."

"How did he know she was going to have twins?"

Maryd shrugged, saying, "I don't know, he just did. But after they were born, as soon as all the blood and brych were washed away, Bridget, just like he said she must do, rubbed each one of her babies from head to foot with a special salve of birch ash and rosemary mixed with her own spittle."

"Oh, my! Did it work?"

"Well the boy child, Bridget named him Ayrn, took immediately to her breast. But she held off naming the girl babe. That one would not stop screaming. That baby clenched her eyes tight shut and beat her tiny fists in the air like she was fighting off some terrible demon." Pantomiming the baby's behavior, Maryd scrunched her eyes closed, clenched her fists, and let out a piercing scream.

Lydia's hands shot to cover her ears as she mouthed, "How awful."

"It was horrible," said Maryd. "Bridget and the wet nurse couldn't do anything to comfort that little girl babe. I wanted to help, but was useless. Then, when Bridget was nearly out of her mind, she remembered the last bit of Mabonig's instructions."

Mayrd jumped up, raised her arms straight over her head, and let her voice drop to a slow monotone. *"If all else fails, Nimue's power can ward off the invaders. Call on her."*

Lydia gave a sharp intake of breath, "Did she really pray to the Moon Goddess?"

"Yes!" Maryd exclaimed.

"What happened?"

"Well, as soon as Bridget cried out Nimue's name, a brilliant white light filled the room. It filled me with awe. When I ran to the window, I saw the clouds that must have been blocking the moon drift away." Maryd paused, clutching her hands together over her heart. "We were surrounded by an eerie silence. The little girl babe gave one last whimper and slept."

Lost in memory, Maryd stood quietly for a few moments, then, looking down at Lydia, said, "That's why Bridget named the girl babe Nimue."

Wide-eyed, Lydia said, "My goodness. That is remarkable. How old is she now?"

"Going on three." Turning to look out over the meadow, Maryd sat down again on the huge boulder by her friend. "Remember, you must never ever tell a soul. Never let

Bridget know I told you."

"Oh, Maryd, you know I won't breathe a word."

"So, are you going to visit Mabonig?"

Lydia bent over to pick a large yellow poppy from the carpet of bluebells surrounding their rock. Slowly she pulled the petals off one by one, "I shall go, I shan't go, I shall go, I shan't..." Stopping mid-sentence, she asked, "Do you think Mabonig can tell me what my dream means?"

"For certain he can. But it may be hard to find his house."

"Well, you can show me."

Maryd shook her head and said, "I don't think he'll tell you what your dream means if I'm there. He says when a message from the Otherworld is given to someone, it is for that person's ears alone."

Lydia frowned and asked, "How will I know if he will be home? I don't want to spend all morning searching and find he's not there."

"Oh, if you get there and he's not home, just wait a spell. He will appear."

Pushing back a branch of a low-hanging hawthorn, Lydia came to a bog oozing with black mud and patched over with tall grass. Thorns and dry thistles clung to her long skirt and her clogs were caked with mud. Searching for a fallen log or some kind of solid footing to make her way across the muck, she was surprised to see a small raft tied to a willow tree at water's edge. On the ground beside the raft was a long, lean branch, which had been cut from the willow and shorn clean of leaves. Lydia untied the raft, picked up the makeshift pole, stepped aboard, and slowly bunted her way across the bog, gasping for an occasional quick breath and trying hard to close her nostrils to the stink of rotting roots and putrid water. Reaching the other side, she maneuvered to the edge of a clearing where a small thatched-roof cottage lay nestled in against the woods on the far side. She gave the steering pole a final push, nudged the craft against solid ground and stepped ashore.

While she secured the raft's line to a slender elm, a large red-tailed hawk swooped down so close that one of its wings brushed Lydia's cheek. Startled, she jumped back and watched the bird fly to the top branch of a huge rowan tree at the edge of the clearing. Standing motionless, waiting for her heart to find its normal pace, she swallowed hard and looked around. Across the clearing, the door to the cottage stood open. She walked gingerly across the clearing to the simple thatched structure and peered into its single room. It was empty.

Sitting down on the cottage's front stoop and questioning her sanity for undertaking such a foolhardy mission, Lydia resolved to wait only a few minutes before heading for home. Yet, after the chill and stink of the bog, the sun's warmth on her shoulders and the fresh scent of meadow grass soothed her spirits. She leaned her head back against the wall and closed her eyes, trying hard not to go to sleep; she only wanted to catch a brief rest before the arduous trek home. When she opened her eyes, a short stooped man with a tall walking staff, a long grey beard, ruddy, wrinkled skin, and twinkling, jet-black eyes stood before her. His knee-length trousers, wool socks, sturdy walking shoes, leather jerkin, woolen undershirt, and pointed hat were all the color of mottled leaves.

"Welcome, Lydia. I am pleased to see you."

Lydia jumped up, blurting out, "How did you know my name?" Then, remembering her manners, "Oh, I beg your pardon. I mean, you surprised me so. I mean, I mean..."

Mabonig laughed. "Sit down, my child. I make it a practice to know the name of everyone in my region. Why, I've watched you from the day you were born. I am so glad that we finally, formally meet."

"But I don't believe I have ever seen you before in my life."

"Ah, perhaps not in the form I take today, but we have been together many times over the years. I recognized you immediately when you came upon my clearing. I'm sorry I gave you a fright."

"Oh, my goodness. You don't mean... Oh, you mean the red-tailed hawk?"

"Why yes, that is one of my favorite garbs."

"Oh." Lydia could think of nothing more to say.

"Won't you sit down? There on the bench under the birch." He pointed to the tall tree with silver bark and small emerald-colored leaves growing by the side of the cottage. "Would you like a cup of tea?"

"Oh, thank you. That would be very nice."

Mabonig stepped into his cottage, and Lydia was barely seated on the narrow plank straddled between two well-matched stones when he reappeared with two mugs of steaming tea and a plate of Bara Brith, Lydia's favorite sweet.

"Now, what brings you to my place on this lovely April morn?"

Lydia took a sip from her mug. She never before had tasted anything as heavenly. As the pungent, sweet, soothing tea slipped down her throat, her previous apprehension melted into calm confidence.

Without hesitation she said, "Well, sir, a few nights ago I had a dream. It seemed like an important dream at the time. I don't know, but it was really strange. I can't keep from thinking about it."

Lydia took another sip of tea, enjoying the little man's hospitality and his interest in her story. "My friend Maryd, she's my very best friend. We've known each other since we were babes. Her parents are cottagers on my father's farm. We live really close. Anyway, you helped her sister when she was going to have twins and..." Lydia stopped in mid-sentence and caught her breath, wondering if Maryd meant she couldn't tell the Wizard. Was she betraying her best friend's trust? But that didn't make any sense. How else would she know about him? Anyway, it was too late now, so she continued, "Maryd said you could tell me what it means. I mean, you could tell me what my dream means. It seems so important. I saw things I've never seen before, there was this beautiful light, amazing, incredibly brilliant, then all went dark and I was falling, and, and..." Lydia heard her words tumbling out, all in a jumble. She took a deep breath to try to stay the torrent.

Mabonig patted her small hand, half the size of his.

"Yes, I remember Bridget. I'm delighted the twins are doing so well. Isn't it lovely that they will have a little brother in June of next year?" Lydia silently counted the months on her fingers. June was over a year away. Bridget couldn't even be pregnant yet. How could he know? But she said nothing.

Mabonig said, "Now, tell me about your dream."

Lydia set her cup down and took a deep breath, slowly puffing it out before she began.

"I was in a big bird's nest high, high in a treetop. I think there were others in the nest, but I'm not sure. All I remember is feeling very happy and very secure when a dazzling yellow light nearly blinded me and a huge eagle with powerful wings swooped down and plucked me out of the nest with his long talons. It did not hurt, and I don't think I was frightened; in fact, it was really exciting to fly way above the treetops and see the woodlands, meadows, and lakes from so high up. Wonderful. But then, as we were flying over our village, the light dimmed, like we'd flown into a huge thundercloud. It was pitch dark, and torrential rain, lightning, and violent winds tossed us about. I couldn't see where we were going and was terribly frightened. Then I was falling down, down, down. The eagle must have lost his grip on me. I can't remember what happened next—you know how dreams are, so confusing—but before I woke up, the eagle was again lifting me high. We were flying toward that same beautiful light, but this time, I was riding on the eagle's back, flying over a vast sea of turbulent water that seemed to go on forever. Then I woke up."

After asking a few questions, Mabonig scratched his chin, tilted his cup to drain out the last drop, and set the cup on the ground. Clasping his knurled fingers together, he looked directly into Lydia's hazel eyes and said, "Lydia, you are correct. This is an important dream. But today I will not tell you what it means. You are not ready. When one learns the future too soon, she tries to take control of what is for God's hands alone. The full meaning of your dream will be revealed to you in time. When you are ready. Do you understand?"

Terribly disappointed Lydia started to protest, but as she looked into the quiet sternness of Mabonig's owl-like face, she realized he would not be swayed. She took a deep breath and murmured a faint, "Yes, sir," but could not resist adding, "Oh please, can't you give me just one little hint?"

Mabonig smiled and gave a nod. "Lydia, my little one, although you will forget your dream for awhile, here is your hint. In your dream, you were surrounded by a beautiful golden light. That light is your guide. Open your heart and find courage. Right now your soul is like a tiny seed, and like a seed, it lies buried deep in fertile soil, in a dark place struggling to grow, to develop, to put down strong roots. As it reaches for the light, it must push hard to work its way around rocks and larger roots; many barriers may block its way, and when it finally bursts forth into light, it will be tender and easily trampled. But, surrounded by and infused with that beautiful golden glow, it will grow and in many ways be transformed."

Mabonig rose and gently placed one of his hands atop her head. His touch, his words, somehow reassured her. "Lydia, you must go now. You soon will enter into a time of young love and newfound pleasures. Enjoy. You shall forget your dream for a while, but take my words to heart. Your dream, your message from God, will be lost to you until you are ready. One day you will remember your dream and look back to understand that it has been fulfilled."

CHAPTER TWO

Parliament...may not tolerate erring consciences, nor false doctrines, any more than they may suffer idolatry.
> —The Scottish Dove (Scots' newspaper in England)
> 11 March 1645

September 26ᵗʰ 1681

As the distant golden orb slipped slowly beneath the clouds hovering above the huge dome of rock to the west, brilliant fingers of orange, vermilion, and pink reached toward the sky and Lydia marveled at the silence of the moment. It was her favorite time of day at the end of her favorite season. In this rosy afterglow of the setting sun, a single swallow-tailed kite, her visible link to the realm she knew existed but could not see, flew in grand circles high above. Lydia sat on the back stoop of the foursquare stone farmhouse, breathing in the scent of lavender soon to be blown asunder by freezing winds as she gently pulled her light shawl securely around her nursing baby. She hummed softly. *"Huna blentyn yn fy mynews, Clyd a chynnes ydw hon; Breichiau mam sy'n dyn am danat, Cariad Mam sy dan fy mron* (Sleep my baby, at my breast, 'Tis a mother's arms round you. Make yourself a snug, warm nest. Feel my love forever new.)"

Rocking back and forth, Lydia hoped to calm her mounting anxiety. Where was he? Why did he not come? Little Rebecca would be asleep soon. Should she go inside, join the rest of the family, re-warm John's supper? Where was he? Usually home well before sunset, this was the third time in a week that John, was late. Gnawing fear tugged for Lydia's attention; she tried hard to push it away, silently reiterating the verse she desperately wanted to believe—*the Lord watches over those who trust in him.* But it was increasingly impossible for her not to be overwhelmed with panic for the safety of her righteous, headstrong husband, so like his father. *Oh God, don't let him end up like his father, a good man, who spent six months in jail because of his beliefs. Why must the Evans men be so openly defiant? Does not their lust for independence put their family, all of us in danger? Where was John?*

Tightening her arms around her now sleeping babe, Lydia stood to pace the length of the narrow planked porch. Back and forth. Back and forth. The soft soles of the house shoes she had put on after her forage in the garden earlier that afternoon barely made a sound. Only the soft swish of her long flannel skirt against the porch railing and an occasional mew from the sleeping babe interrupted the evening hush.

At last, a distant bark broke the silence; straining her eyes through the gathering dusk, Lydia caught first sight of a small, barely distinguishable dot on the horizon. Uttering a swift prayer of gratitude, the vise squeezing her heart relaxed a bit as she watched the dark, lumbering shape transform into the tall, lanky body of her husband sitting slouched in the saddle on his grey mare. Cin, their small, low slung, black and white corgi, scampered on the trail before the horse and rider heralding their homecoming.

When John reached the house, he sat slumped with his feet dangling out of the stirrups before slowly dismounting and stretching his long legs, giving each foot a sluggish shake. Standing beside his horse, supporting himself with one hand on the saddle horn, he looked over at Lydia, who now stood on the bottom step of the porch, and said in a low voice, "Lydia, my love, shouldn't you and the little one be inside by the fire? The air grows chilled."

Searching his face, ashen with fatigue, Lydia noted the depth of the lines creasing his normally smooth brow. She hesitated, but was compelled to speak, "John. John dear, I was worried. You are so late."

In unhurried deliberation, John wrapped the horse's reins around the yard post and stepped onto the porch, "Ah, my dear Lydia, do sit down. We must talk."

In spite of her apprehension, Lydia felt relief. Was John finally going to take her into his confidence? For weeks he had been unwilling to share his concerns, replacing his normal vitality with awkward silence, like a heavy fog permeating the atmosphere when they were together. The open, easy sharing of the most trivial, mundane thoughts, as well as their most intimate feelings, was what had attracted her to John over the other young men who had come courting three years back. Oh too, there was that unexpected, unexplainable flip her stomach made when she spotted him behind the plough in a distant field or walking across the road toward her. John was good-looking, a little over six feet

tall with a strong, lean body, broad shoulders, hay-colored
hair that matched the eyebrows bleached nearly white by
the sun, and big, round blue eyes. There was something else
too. When she was with him she felt completely absorbed in
a kind of powerful goodness. He was quiet, thoughtful, slow
to express his opinion, but when he spoke, she trusted every
word he said; when she accepted his proposal for marriage,
his heart opened to her and a torrent of words poured forth as
he shared his every hope and dream for their future together.
But, about a month ago, everything changed. His words, like
their meadow stream in last year's drought, dried up.

Three nights ago, after they had climbed into bed, before
blowing out the candle, she had mustered her courage and
asked, "John, what troubles you? Can you not tell me?"

Slowly shaking his head, he lay still for long moments
before responding, "Oh Lydia, my mind is too confused. I
shan't burden you with such confusion. I shall not speak until I understand more." Lifting her chin, he had placed a soft
kiss on her lips. "Please bear with me for a while longer. I
pray constantly for guidance, for clarity." Disheartened, but
knowing she could not penetrate the wall he had erected until he opened the gate, she blew out the candle and snuggled
into his arms.

Now as she settled herself on the porch bench with little
Rebecca in her lap, John spoke softly but with firmness.
"Lydia, I am convinced our future can no longer be in this
cherished land of our fathers."

Immediately on her feet, Lydia wrapped one arm around
his lean body while holding the sleeping babe in the other

and countered, "John..,John, why now? What has happened?
What are you saying? Surely our faith will sustain us."

John's body stiffened. He did not return her embrace.
Thrusting his hands into the deep pockets of his leather jerkin
he shook his head. "They are bent on destroying us. The
new sheriff has proven to be far worse than that intolerable
Puritan Vavasor Powell." John puffed his cheeks and let out
a low sigh. "Today an edict was posted, declaring that pen-
alties for refusal to sign the oath of allegiance are to be even
muy dieflig. Much harsher, longer prison terms, the severest
of punishments." In spite of his obvious fatigue, John was
energized by giving voice to long pent-up emotions. His
voice rose, his words clipped forth in rapid succession, brash,
rhetorical, as if he were standing before a large crowd instead
of an audience of two—his diminutive wife and their sleeping
babe. "Even now, you know that one of ours cannot hold
public office, and marriage vows taken outside the established Church are not recognized as legal." Startled at the
brashness of his own voice, John paused, swallowed hard,
touched a finger to the soft cheek of his sleeping daughter, and
continued in a softer tone, "In the eyes of the law of the land,
our little Rebecca and all our children to come are bastards."

Standing stolidly before the small figure of his wife,
he watched her calm determination attempt to mask her
growing anguish. Lydia's ancestral roots coiled deeply into
Maesyfed, the small section of south central Wales renamed
Radnorshire by English overlords during the last century.
She loved her land; she cherished childhood memories of
rambling through the woods with her grandfather, hearing

stories about their people and their land—this land that linked her to a noble, magical past. Her soul was tied to this place. Even today, although unfaltering in her newly adopted Quaker faith, she never passed the four Druid stones near the church yard in Old Radnor without stopping to soak in their sanctity. She loved the beautiful, golden glow emanating from those hard, worn stones like a halo of sunshine and was surprised when she mentioned this ethereal aura to others that no one else saw it.

Now looking up into John's face, Lydia saw pain. He, too, was deeply connected to this land, firmly tied to its gentle hills and pastures. The land John shared with his father was the land his father had shared with his father before him. Fathers and sons had lived and worked this land as far back as memory reached.

Her words were barely audible, "Why now? Will not these bad times pass?"

"Lydia, we all know that the misery for our people started under Cromwell, but it is growing far worse with the restoration of King Charles, thousands of our brethren suffer imprisonment." John placed his large hands on Lydia's shoulders and stared down into her hazel eyes. "Is this the life you want for our children? Where does their future lie? How can we live in bonds of such intolerance?"

Lydia gave a slight shrug and gazed down at the babe in her arms. "I thought with the restoration of King Charles we would again know toleration and could worship in peace."

Dropping his hands to his side, John's retort was instantaneous, "It is obvious that his persecution is a hundred-

fold harsher than that of Puritan Cromwell. This morning
Sister Adwen told me that our saintly leader Brother Fox
was immediately arrested and jailed on his return from the
New World." John lowered his head and gave a barely audible
utterance, "The Lord is testing our will beyond anything I
ever imagined."

After standing in silence for a few moments, Lydia said
gently, "Come, John, you must eat. I'll go warm your supper
while you feed and brush down Cynwar and wash at the
well. Then we will talk."

Baby Rebecca slept soundly by the large stone hearth in
a small cradle crafted from a single branch of knurled hazel-
wood; the other members of the household gathered along
each side of the kitchen table, a long, worn plank of oak set
on trestles. The room was filled with the aroma of mutton
and leeks, the last serving of the week's pottage held warm in
the small pottery pipkin nestled on the embers at the edge of
the hearth. John, having washed the day's dirt and swat from
his neck and face, sat down, worn but composed, his broad
shoulders bent with fatigue. Lydia, sitting on the bench next
to the fire an arm's length from Rebecca's cradle, which she
occasionally nudged into a gentle rock, reached over and
spooned the contents of the pipkin onto a plate and placed
it before her husband saying, "Eat well, John."

"Thank you, dear wife," John said as he bowed his head
in a silent prayer of gratitude before picking up his fork.

At the end of the table sat John ap Evan, John's father.
The lower right side of his once handsome face was covered

by an angry keloid scar, his useless right hand lay limp in his lap, and a crutch was propped at the back of his chair. Opposite Lydia sat John's mother, Elizabeth, large boned and sturdy, a good-looking woman still trim at forty-three. Mother Elizabeth's long narrow face, typical of the western moorland folk, was said to be traceable to the original pre-history people who came to Wales from no-one-knew where. Sitting on either side of Elizabeth were her other two children, eighteen-year-old Tom, a couple of inches shorter than the six feet of his older brother, John, and fourteen-year-old Liz, whose curly red hair and long chin mirrored that of her mother's. Twin brothers, born between Tom and Liz, had died when the scourge of smallpox ravished nearly every family in the shire seven years before.

Waiting for John to finish his supper, his father knocked the used tobacco from his clay pipe and remarked, "I hope the weather holds until you get the fields cut. Nos Calan Gaeaf is fast upon us." Turning to his younger son, he asked, "How far did you get today, Tom?"

A wide smile lit Tom's freckled face. "Nearly finished the lower pasture behind the barn. We should be able to bring in all the hay within three days."

Elizabeth nodded, saying, "That is good news. All signs are that we shall have our first frost anytime now."

John drained the final draught from his pewter tankard, pushed his plate away, pulled a large homespun kerchief from a back pocket, and wiped his mouth. Turning to each of the women folk around the table in turn, he said, "Thank you, Mother, thank you wife, thank you Little Liz, 'twas excellent fare." Then, turning back to his mother added, "Though I must admit that sallet of bardock roots is not one of my favorites."

"Why, John, you know a bit of savory is essential for your digestion," retorted Elizabeth.

Looking directly into his mother's huge blue eyes, the mirror image of his own, he gave a broad grimace, then a wink but said nothing more. The family fell silent, waiting. Knowing that John wanted time to gather his thoughts, they all sat with bowed heads until he was ready. Several minutes passed before John turned to his father and nodded. John ap Evan, looked around the table, studying the countenance of each individual—hope mingled with more than a little fear was writ large on every face. In a voice reflecting conviction but calm resignation, he said, "Let us ask for the Lord's light to guide us in these matters that weigh heavy on our hearts."

As Elizabeth bowed her head, memories of those fateful days, five years past, flashed before her. She tried to push them away. Now was not the time. She wanted to block out those uninvited recollections—her heated arguments with her husband late into the night after the children had gone to bed, the tearful charges she had fired, one on top of the other, giving him no time to respond. "Why, John? Why must you place yourself in such jeopardy? Can you not think of me? Have you completely forgotten your children? Are they not sacred too? What shall become of us?" She had made harsh, screeching accusations, all the time knowing that her words seared him to his core. Her husband was not a selfish man. He was a good man. She knew that above all else John ap Evan believed that with his every breath he must be true to their loving God. Every act, word, and relationship must demonstrate his allegiance to the teachings of Jesus. Her husband lived his belief. Elizabeth shuddered remembering the bitter remonstrations that had poured forth from her lips.

Now, five years later, her most fervent desire was to swallow them back. The elder John's response had been slow, labored, barely audible. "I cannot, I will not, degrade myself before my Maker. I can never live falsely or show even a modicum of respect to an undeserving, arrogant fool, full of fatuous airs of self importance." Her husband had pleaded, "Elizabeth, please try to understand. To feign deference to values I abhor is dishonest...blasphemy." He had reached for her hand, pulled her to him, begging her to understand. She had not understood and had turned her stiffened back and said nothing more.

Later that week, the elder John had been arrested for not removing his hat in the presence of the shire's ruling nobleman, Lord Manchet, the Earl of Newbury. Lord Manchet had been incensed. He believed, as did most all noblemen, that any breach in the established rules for honoring one's superiors could not be tolerated; such behavior was a direct affront to the authority of all English nobility and, by association, to King Charles himself. However, when John ap Evan was brought before the Radnorshire court, the judge said he would release him, give John ap Evan another chance if he would confess his error and sign an oath of allegiance to the Crown. Elizabeth remembered standing at the back of the courtroom during her husband's arraignment, knowing his response before he said a word. John ap Evan refused both demands. He would not admit error and swore he would never sign an oath of allegiance to the King. His allegiance was to be given only to his Father in Heaven.

The judge sitting behind the high walnut bench had pulled himself to his full height, struck his gavel hard on the platform before him, and decreed in accusatory, sententious tones that, "Men who will not swear allegiance to civil or ecclesiastic authority are a dangerous threat to the order of the realm. The peace of England, the stability of our country, depends on dousing the flames of all renegade nonconformists." Pausing to stare directly at John ap Evan, who met his gaze with calm equanimity, the judge continued, "As representative of our noble King Charles II, the Church of England, and the hope for civility and peace in our fair land, I am convinced that you non-conforming Quakers need to be taught a lesson." Again pounding his gavel loudly on the high bench, the judge declared, "You, John ap Evan, shall serve six months in Radnor prison starting today."

Thus, John ap Evan, an independent Welsh farm holder from a long line of independent Welsh farm holders, was thrown into jail along with hardened criminals where he was fed rancid food and made to sleep in his own and others' excrement. After the prescribed six months of periodic beatings, he was released a physically broken man, scarred and crippled but with an unwavering conviction that a man must never swear allegiance to anyone but God. No man or government would dictate John ap Evan's relationship to his Maker. Freedom of conscience was a man's fundamental right, and no earthly power could take it away.

Her husband's imprisonment was five years ago, and Elizabeth knew she must pull her thoughts back to the present. Now, sitting with her family in contemplative silence in her warm kitchen, she swallowed hard, seeking to calm her heart, still her mind, and open herself to the living spirit. Finally, her son John cleared his throat and quietly declared, "Our life in Maesyfed is no longer tolerable."

Lydia kept her head lowered and her eyes tightly closed, trying to hold back the tears forming beneath her eyelids. Her thoughts trailed across the valley to her mother, her father, her sisters Elian, Haf, and Mali, and her brothers Beli, Barryn, and Bran. Yes, she was John's wife and had accepted a new religion with her marriage vows, but she was also a Cledwyn. Her family of birth was very much a part of her life. How strange it had seemed during the first weeks of marriage to be sharing a bed with a man instead of three giggling sisters. She still walked the mile and a half across the valley at least twice a week to tease and gossip with her siblings, but her husband's next words brought Lydia abruptly back into her new family's kitchen, "Our only hope is to join our brethren now in America."

Tom exclaimed, "I saw Garth in the village yesterday, and he told me of a letter that came last week from his cousin. He says their family prospers and worships freely in the new world."

John, knowing that his declaration would receive enthusiastic endorsement from his younger brother, ever keen for adventure, smiled and said, "Yes, our brothers and sisters of faith have established a foothold across the seas and..." John paused to look for a moment around the table, appreciating the rapt but nervous attention he saw in each face. "At our meeting last night I learned of even greater opportunity. The King repaying a debt owed to William Penn's father has given Brother Penn a huge parcel of land in the new country—millions of acres. Brother Penn has proclaimed—" John stopped abruptly, lifted his chin and gave a slight dramatic tilt to his head before pronouncing each word slowly and distinctly, "It shall be a colony of toleration. A holy experiment. A place where true believers will live in peace, directed only by Christ Jesus and their own inner light." He paused to look around the table again, then took a deep breath and said, "Brother Penn is looking for immigrants. I believe we must go."

Reaching under the table, John took Lydia's small hand in his field-roughened palm and was relieved to feel her return his grasp with a firm squeeze. "It is said that Brother William desires to call the colony Sylvania," he continued, "descriptive of the verdant woods that cover all the land. But the King, mindful of the unflagging loyalty and financial support of William's now deceased father, declared that this new colony shall be called Penn's Sylvania."

A near silent ripple spread around the table as the family quietly tested and tasted the name of the place that might be so important to their future. Mother Elizabeth was the first to speak. Shaking her head, her words poured forth in a rush, "Such a venture will take a great deal of forethought and much money. Hasty sales bring little profit and oftentimes much loss. If we decide this course, we must be very prudent in the disposal of our holdings."

John, noting the quiver in his mother's voice, cleared his throat and responded in a low, even tone. He knew the proposed wrench from their land would be exceedingly difficult for his parents. His mother's family's contribution to their livelihood was significant. Her dowry had permitted the marriage of his parents twenty-three years before and had helped pay for five years of schooling for each of their children. Because of his parents' frugality, John, unlike many of the villagers his age, could study the Gospel on his own and read the political tracts distributed around the shire. As a young lad, John had realized his mother, in fact, both his parents were different from most of the folks in their shire; they were very progressive for their times. They not only gave their children an education, but noting the increasing commerce with people beyond their shire and wanting their family to always be able to trace their heritage, his parents broke with tradition and established a surname for the family that would live on from one generation to the next. John ap Evan and Elizabeth added an "s" to John's father's name and created Evans as the surname for their children. When he, their first son, was born in 1660, he was not named John ap John; the birth certificate read John Evans.

However, his parents were tied closely to their land, and their land and their heritage were one. John honored his mother's concern. "Yes, Mother, you speak the truth. Careful planning is essential, but those of our Society who have forged new lives in America show it can be done."

Elizabeth looked down at her hands folded on the table before her and said in a tremulous voice, "But, son, this is

the land of our fathers. Think what we would be leaving. Do
we abandon our heritage? This is not the first trouble that
has wracked our people...and it will not be the last."

The elder John looked at his wife. This strong woman
had shouldered the brunt of daily responsibilities since his
imprisonment, since his battered body could no longer up-
hold his share. She was the family's rock. She had kept their
lives together these past five years. Their sons were, only now,
beginning to relieve her of most of the farm's management.
He said in calm and measured tones, "So true, so true. But
we must weigh our choices carefully. Such a choice may never
have been within the grasp of those who came before us.
This is the land of our ancestors. Our people worked these
fields for themselves at times, and for those who imposed a
rule over them at other times. They did the best they could.
We owe them much." Pausing for emphasis, he continued,
"Yet, it is our souls, not our land, that is of primary concern.
It is our souls, not our land, that connect us to our Lord."
Though his body was broken, his voice bore the timber of his
previous strength. "Now, as ever before, we must prayerfully
listen for guidance as to what is right for us at this time. It
may be time to seek a new place."

Tom, emboldened by his father's speech, blurted out,
"The way things are going, before long we will all probably
be thrown in prison if we stay here."

With blazing eyes, Elizabeth looked up at her young
son. "Tom, don't be loose with your words. Consider well
before you speak. These are serious matters that will not be
decided out of fear for the consequences of our beliefs." Then

turning to her older son, she said, "John, I know this matter
has been heavy on your heart for many months, but you
have until now refrained from speaking out. Please, tell us
all that you can, the reasons for your decision at this time."

John said, "Mother, your grandchildren and, for that
matter, Liz, Tom, and I, according to the new laws are ille-
gitimate bastards. You and father said your marriage vows
within the Society, Lydia and I have done the same. Only
marriages within the Established Church of England are
now considered legal. We and our children have no rights.
What will this do to our claims of inheritance? What will this
do to our lives? Who knows if Father and I will be allowed to
cast a vote in the next election. We cannot hold office. We
have no rights unless we swear our oath to the King."

"That would be blasphemy of the highest order. Our
allegiance is only to our Lord and Savior Jesus Christ," his
father said quietly. John paused to look over at his father's
bowed head and continued, "Tom is right. More than eleven
thousand of our brethren have already seen prison, and the
new laws promise even harsher treatment. Yet, I agree with
you, Mother, we must not act out of fear." Reflecting on
his own words, John paused for such a long time the others
wondered if he had anything more to say. A single muffled
burp from Little Rebecca broke the silence and her father
continued, "I have been praying for months for an answer.
We know that to resist with violence would be against the
will of our Lord. My heart has been deeply confused." John
paused again, swallowed hard, and finally continued in a
slow, measured tone, hoping that his words would sway the

others to his resolve, "But now, with the promise of a place where we can worship freely, live by laws that we and our brethren will make, all seems right and true to me."

Reaching across the table, he placed his large palm over his mother's tightly clenched fists. "Mother, I fervently believe our going to Penn's Sylvania is God's answer." Lydia, still holding John's other hand under the table, was startled by a brilliant flash of golden light, like a star exploding inside her head, but said nothing.

No one spoke for several minutes. Then Elizabeth rose and walked to the head of the table to stand behind her husband and place her hands on his shoulders; she momentarily pressed her lips together and looked directly at her son. "John, you have opened your heart to the Lord and you have received an answer. To watch my children and grandchildren live and worship freely is the greatest gift a woman can know." Lowering her voice, she continued, "I appreciate that you recognize how hard this is for me. I do feel much reluctance in my heart." She took a deep breath and looked up into the ceiling beams before continuing. "I pray as we move forward in this difficult venture, my heart will soften. I am convinced that your decision is the Lord's will." She shook her head slowly and asked, "How do you propose we begin?"

John gazed across the table in admiration, "Thank you for your confidence, Mother. So very much depends on you. Our plans will take the best of all our wits and prayers." Knowing that his father's inability to physically help with preparations, plus realizing that the severity of the journey would be very hard on him, John said, "Father, we look to you to think through the details, organize our labor, and supervise the sale of our property. You bring the necessary experience for such an undertaking." John's father nodded a quiet assent.

Listening to his family discuss the details of this irreversible uprooting of their lives, argue over strategies for the sale of their property, and consider the logistics of immigration, John felt profound gratitude. It was no longer a question of if, but how and when.

Tall candles burned to small nubs as the family gradually came to tentative agreements; it would take at least eighteen months before they could actually leave Maeysfed. The major priority was to find top price for their house, household goods, barn, and the tenant rights of their land; their savings needed to be maximized through the sale of next spring's lambs and summer crops. Although this could most likely be accomplished by the middle of next autumn, the winter months were a dangerous time to set out on such an arduous journey. It would take a day or two to travel by cart to a port on the southern coast, a week for the channel crossing to Holland, and two to three months for the voyage across the turbulent waters of the Atlantic. Yet, as the family diligently listed every conceivable task, assigned responsibilities, and considered possible complications they might confront in the months ahead, they had no way of knowing that intervening events could upset such carefully conceived plans.

CHAPTER THREE

October 2ⁿᵈ 1681

The staccato notes of the rooster's crow, announcing that dawn would come within the hour, pierced the stillness of Lydia's restless vigil. John was not yet home. *God, oh gracious Father, be with him. Protect him. Do not forsake him. Oh, God.* Her heart tightened. Every muscle in her body was taut as her words froze on her lips. She drew her knees to her chest and pressed her forehead into her pillow's rough linen covering. This regal-size bolster, filled with goose down she had plucked and cleaned two springs past in anticipation of John's handsome head resting beside hers, now bore the weight of her mounting fear. Exhausted from a sleepless night after weeks of ceaseless worry, Lydia, curled tightly with her knees pressing into her chin, finally drifted into troubled sleep.

The night before, as the family finished supper, John had whispered to Lydia, "Please come outside for a moment."

He then excused himself, bid a hasty farewell to the others, and put on his light overcoat and broad-brimmed black hat. Lydia, quickly at his side, grabbed a rough woolen shawl off the hook by the back door and followed him into the brisk night air. John was going to a secret meeting of the Friends where Joshua Jones, a fellow Quaker recently returned from the new world settlement in the Delaware Valley, would speak. The meeting was being held deep in the woods after dark, and as a safeguard against arousing the suspicions of nosy neighbors trying to curry favor with the authorities, only one man from each household was going to the gathering. John was eager to attend this particular meeting. He wanted to talk with someone who had actually immigrated to America, someone who had accomplished what his family planned to do. He needed names of contacts and locations of meeting places of Friends along the way in southern Wales, Holland, and America, information about safe harbors, shipping schedules, costs, warnings about unanticipated pitfalls. He also wanted to start looking for a potential buyer for their property.

Once outside and alone, John wrapped Lydia in his arms, nuzzling his chin against the white, starched house bonnet covering her long chestnut locks. They both knew he should not linger, yet the two clung together in silent prayer, a secure oasis of love in the tumultuous field of danger. There was always the possibility of him being observed and followed. These days, every parting between loved ones within their Society of Friends was charged with unspoken dread. Their faith placed them in constant jeopardy of arrest. They learned the difficult lesson that strong faith did not remove fear; it only gave them courage to act in spite of their fear.

It was a three-quarters of an hour walk to the small clearing deep in Radnor Woods where the meeting tent was secretly erected. John planned to take a circuitous route to mislead anyone who might see him on the road. He wanted to avoid any possibility of being followed so would not go directly to the clearing. Not until he was positive that he was not observed would he head into the woods. A chance observance by a neighbor loyal to the King not only jeopardized his safety but the safety of his brethren gathered at the meeting.

Pushing away from his firm chest, Lydia had whispered, "John dear, it is past time that you should be off." As he reluctantly released her from his arms, she said, "Be careful, dear husband. God is with you. Your bed will be warm on your return." He stooped to kiss her upturned lips and strode out into the deepening shadows of the October night. Their small corgi, Cin, who had been pawing at John's leg, began to follow his master before Lydia ran to scoop the little dog into her arms and take him into the house. Cin barked at the least provocation, and would not be a good partner in stealth.

The designated meeting spot, a small clearing well back into Radnor Forest halfway between the north and south branches of the Lug River, was northwest of the their property. After leaving Lydia, John headed due south toward the village, sauntering at an even pace and looking intently to see whether there was anyone in front or behind him. He saw no one. He also kept a sharp eye on the adjacent fields, thankful that these fields had been cut last week, the shorn grass made it easier to spot someone in the gathering dusk. A slight breeze caused John to look to the sky where he noted the dark cluster of clouds gathering in the west. Rain was on the way. It would be a wet night.

Heading south, it was a ten-minute walk to the Llewelyns, the closest household along the road. The Llewelyns were good enough people, but not members of the Society of Friends, and John was uncertain of their loyalties. Passing their house with measured strides, he noted that the place looked locked up for the night. With no one in the yard among the out-buildings, the family was probably gathered for supper in the back kitchen of the main house. In any event, John figured that if someone were peering from a window, it would appear that he was heading into New Radnor, perhaps for an evening brew with the men folk. Keeping the same even pace, he continued up the road and topped the steep hill just beyond the Llewelyns'. After starting down its other side, and well out of sight of any buildings, he stopped abruptly and looked in all directions. Certain that there were no prying eyes about, John stepped off the road. The wind was picking up, so he secured the top button on his coat, turned up his collar, and pulled his hat securely down to his ears before beginning his trot directly across the field toward the woods of Radnor Forest.

Radnor Forest drew him in like a magnet. No other place on earth spoke so directly of the brave inheritance John claimed as a son of this land. Even though he and all his kinfolk were soon to leave this place, John knew that this large unenclosed plateau of rock and woods would always be a part of him. The history and spirit of his people were rooted solidly in this soil along with the giant oaks and rowans.

Soon darkness would encompass all, and with no moon, once he reached the protection of the underbrush and trees, he could proceed undetected. John Evans was not the first Welshman to seek sanctuary in this primeval terrain. As a young lad, John had roamed its woods and hillocks hoping to find a remnant of chipped stone or flint used by a prehistoric Celt in the far distant past. In later years, hunting for game in the quiet wooded areas of the forest or fishing along the shores of its many streams, he quietly connected to his proud Welsh heritage. The untamed woods of Radnor Forest had been a haven for his freedom-loving people through all the ages past. And now, in the dim light, its towering trees created a giant, swaying mass of dark, a protective veil for him and his brethren. John's every sense quickened with the rising wind as sharp pelts of rain stung his cheeks. Never before had he felt so drawn to this sacrosanct place. The forest's unseen forces were drawing him into its fold; past generations of Welshmen were calling, frantically urging, *brisio*, John, hurry.

Still beautiful in its primordial splendor, magnificent Radnor Forest, the hunting ground, the sanctuary throughout the ages for all true Welshmen, was calling him. John heard a cacophony of sound. Voices of his ancestors urging him forward into their asylum, a safe place to hide, a place to gather courage, courage to deal with those who threatened his liberty, his independence, his life. He heard strange, unfamiliar harmonies of first century Celts, who took refuge in the forest's craggy hills, refusing to give allegiance to the invading Roman legionnaires who occupied much of Britain for over four hundred years. As the chorus grew louder, he detected new voices, speaking what sounded like his native tongue, but with a different accent, other words; he somehow knew that this was the early medieval dialect of the descendents of those ancient Celts. The rhythm and inflections were different, but the meaning was the same—defiant dedication to a life of liberty for themselves and for their families. These new voices told of Anglo Saxon marauders from the north who drove out the Romans in the fifth century and established rule over most of the British Isles for another five hundred years. But not in Radnor Forest. The Welsh lands of John's ancestors held strong and independent.

A crisp blast of trumpets heralding his approach made his heart leap. John recognized the sound. King Arthur was summoning him to his grounds. King Arthur, that valiant and benevolent eighth century champion for all of Britain, the personification of John's peoples' glorious traditions, was here to greet him. This was Arthur's land. Arthur's legendary capitol Camelot, ancient Caereleon, was but a half days ride from Radnor Forest. Had not Arthur come to Old Radnor to fetch his young bride Guinevere? Displayed on all Arthurian battle banners was the magnificent Red Dragon, the Celtic symbol of courage and justice. The very dragon that was said to be sleeping still, deep in Radnor Forest. The small church about five hundred yards from the Evans' back pasture was one of four churches built several hundred years before to contain that fabulous winged serpent in its woodland lair.

Reaching the first line of trees, protected now from the wind and rain, John stopped to catch his breath. The ringing in his ears, those echoes from the past, stopped with him. He lingered but half a minute and, with purposeful strides amongst the shadows, reached the meeting spot in less than a quarter of an hour.

A small group, nine of John's kith, sat quietly, cross-legged on the ground around a well-shaded lantern under a small, hastily constructed lean-to tent. All heads were bowed. John slipped down beside Brother Arn, lowering his eyes to clear his mind. He knew everyone in the group except the middle-aged fellow with a brush of red hair sprouting from beneath his broad-brimmed hat. That must be Joshua Jones.

Brother Arn looked up, cleared his throat, and said, "The Lord be with you." The others responded in unison, "And also with you." Arn continued in a soft, deep voice that carried authority, "Knowing the danger that each of us take on ourselves and our families, we will proceed directly to the business at hand and welcome Brother Joshua Jones who immigrated to America over ten years past and is back in Wales to visit his family in Aberffram. The ship for his return voyage leaves from Leyden in seven days, and we are fortunate that he passes through Radnor on his journey south." Arn nodded and smiled at the stranger. "We are most eager to hear your report on life in America. Thank you and God bless you for coming to us, Brother Jones."

Joshua Jones remained seated as his dark eyes, set in a sun-creased face, deliberately connected with each man in the circle before he spoke. "Thank you, brothers. Of course, we all are cognizant of the ever present threat from the king's men to each of you, a threat, thank the Lord, we in our Society of Friends do not experience in our new land across the sea." The solemn tone of his words lightened as he continued. "It is always a pleasure to be among my friends in faith. I am eager to share all that I can about my life in the new world." Pausing a moment to collect his thoughts, he stroked his long beard and said, "Since our time together is limited, I believe the best way to proceed is for you to ask questions. I will try to answer. That way I will not burden you with information that may be of no value, or that you already know."

Everyone spoke at once: "Is the good land taken?" "What will be the cost of the voyage?" "Which parts are best for settlement?" "What about the Indians?" "What about the weather?" "Do you have to know how to speak English to get along?" "Will we be persecuted for our faith?"

Under the barrage of questions, Joshua Jones raised his right hand above his head, gave a slight wave, and brought the index finger of his other hand across his lips. "Brothers, perhaps we best take one question at a time, each in turn around the circle. But before we begin, I must emphasize that your first and most important step in the arduous undertaking of immigration is to put your trust in our dear Lord's protection. He is our light. He is your guide." Joshua Jones then turned to the man sitting to his right, "My brother, what is it you would like to hear from me?"

Aaeron Fultermore looked up, gave a nervous tug on his long beard, and stuttered, "Wh-wh-wh-what i-i-i-is the b-b-b-b-b-best p-p-p-place?"

Joshua Jones, put his hand on Aaeron's shoulder, "Ah, I believe the best place for a Society Member to settle is somewhere in the vicinity of our small community of Friends in the Delaware Valley. And now, with the King's land grant to William Penn, who is eager to populate his territory with Friends, that area between the small village of Chester and the main port at Philadelphia will be especially attractive. Plenty of good farm land and a well-protected harbor close by." Slowly shaking his head, Jones continued, "It's amazing the growth the area has seen in only ten years."

"What was it like when you first got there?" asked the fellow next to Aaeron.

"Well, when the wife and I landed with our three boys, we now have seven, the first two years were mighty difficult —unceasing work, hard work, felling trees, clearing land, planting our first crops, eking out enough to eat, building simple houses, tending the sick, burying the dead." Jones took off his hat, drew a red kerchief from a jacket pocket, and wiped his brow before replacing his hat; just describing those years seemed to tire him. "But that's why it is so important to be among brothers. Our small band of Friends always was there to help one another."

"Are you truly able to worship in peace?" asked Dylan Arwel.

"Absolutely. Above all else, the privilege to worship God in freedom made it well worth the hardships."

Again Jones paused to hear the next question, "What about the natives?"

"In our area, the native Indians, the Lenne Lenape, are a peaceful, friendly tribe. They were a tremendous help from the very first. They showed us good hunting grounds, the wild fruit and herbs that were edible, the closest spots to quarry rocks for our wells and house foundations."

Someone interrupted, "What about fresh water?"

"Pure and plentiful. There is an abundance of rain and the streams are loaded with trout."

"Any other folk around?" another man asked.

"Some Swedes and other immigrants came to the area and settled around the neighboring harbor about thirty years ago, but folks don't bother much with one another. Everyone holds to his or her own ways and believes in a give-and-take kind of living."

John said, " Sounds like a paradise of tolerance, so different from what we know here."

Joshua Jones quickly retorted, "Well, I've heard that not all areas in America are as accepting of others' beliefs as our Delaware Valley. Several years ago, two of our Quaker sisters, traveling ministers talking tolerance and the equality of women and men before God, were hung up in Boston for their preaching." Scratching his chin and looking once again around the circle, Jones said, "You probably will want to avoid the Massachusetts Colony. Though the soil is fertile and the Boston harbor flourishes with commercial activity, the Puritans of that colony countenance no deviation in word or deed from their established rules and doctrine."

A voice on the far side of the circle muttered. "Those Puritans be the same the world over."

When asked about the Atlantic crossing, Jones slowly nodded his head, "Yes, the voyage across the ocean was long and difficult.

The quarters below deck were extremely crowded, impossible to find even a nook for privacy. The air was rank, and no matter how fastidious our attempt at cleanliness, a squalid living space was inevitable. The food was scarce and sometimes rancid. I lost almost three stones in the crossing." Jones again took off his hat and wiped his brow with his red kerchief. "Dreadful storms...constant rocking makes a stomach wrench. During the rough seas, there's no walking about...at times, even standing upright is impossible." Here he gave a deep sigh and a slight smiled crossed his lips. "But...after the storm passes, the fresh clean air on deck charges one's soul. You feel the Lord's blessings shower down directly from heaven."

The questioning continued for over an hour, and John was about to ask what he should budget for his family's boat passage when he heard shouting in the distance, the tromping of feet, and the barking of dogs.

The light in the center of the circle was quickly doused and the men quietly fanned out in all directions, knowing that, at this point, it was every man for himself. The rain had stopped and the woods were dead quiet save for footfalls of the advancing king's men. A barn owl hooted above as John slipped from tree to bush, holding close to the shadows, relying on his ears to avoid detection and his keen sense of direction and familiarity with the woods to lead him to safety.

CHAPTER FOUR

October 3rd 1681

B am. Bam. Bam. Terrorized by the pounding, the unceasing plaint of the iron mallet striking nails into the large pine box, Lydia struggled to reach the horny hand that wielded the offending hammer. But her arms and legs, were bound tight, immobilized, as an unseen force drew her down, down, down.

Bam. Bam. Bam. She woke with a start. Disoriented from her dream, she fought to bring her world into focus. Where was John? How long had she slept?

Bam. Bam. Bam. Rays of early morning light streamed through the high window of their second-story bedchamber. Her head throbbed in rhythm with the incessant sound coming from below. Who? What? As her feet searched to find the floor, fear stiffened every joint in her body, yet she somehow managed to pull on her light woolen wrapper and scramble down the narrow stairs. The stones of the first floor paving were cold under her bare feet.

Lifting the heavy latch, Lydia pushed the door open. An imposing figure, surrounded by early morning mist rising from the moors, filled the opening. "Mistress Evans?" a gruff, heavy voice inquired.

"Aye, that is my name."

"Your husband is being held in the jail in New Radnor."

All was going blank, near black. Lydia felt her knees start to buckle as she reached out to place the palm of her hand against the open entranceway to steady herself; but the demands of continual fear and restless nights were too much on her body in the first month of a pregnancy she suspected but had not yet confirmed. As Lydia slumped to the floor, Mother Elizabeth, tall and formidable with a streak of gray at her brow, appeared and addressed the man standing on the threshold.

"What is it that brings you here at this Godforsaken hour, young man?"

"I come to inform the lady that her husband has broken the peace and lies in Radnor prison."

"Ah, so now that you have delivered your message, be off." The older woman slammed the heavy door closed with a trembling hand.

Elizabeth bent down to touch the brow of the inert figure that lay at her feet and examine Lydia's head to make sure that the fall had not split her skull. Seeing no blood, Elizabeth hastened to the kitchen, snatched the shawl, the same grey and blue tartan Lydia had used the night before, grabbed a tin beaker from the table and ran to the well behind the house. She lowered the oaken bucket and cranked it up full of pure, sparkling water, which she too quickly poured into the tall beaker, causing a great splash to land atop her left foot. Ignoring the frigid discomfort, the older woman raced as quickly as her stiffened joints would move back to her daughter-in-law, who lay unmoving on the stone floor within. Kneeling beside the still figure, Elizabeth took a soft cloth and gently doused the unconscious girl's face and neck with cold water, felt her pulse, and smoothed her hair. Within minutes, Lydia's eyes began to flutter, and Elizabeth raised her daughter-in-law's head and touched a cup of the icy, fresh water to her lips.

"Easy now, take but a small sip at first."

Lydia, disoriented, murmured softly, "Thank you, Mother Elizabeth. Where am I?"

"You are safe with me. There's no rush, but when you feel the strength to move, you must go the kitchen to sit beside the fire. Little Rebecca will be waking and wanting her breakfast."

Lydia's eyes opened wide and she gave a startled gasp when she realized that she lay sprawled on the hard field stones of the front hall. She struggled to sit up and then, leaning on her mother-in-law, allowed the older woman to pull her to her feet. She swayed within the other woman's strong encircling arm and shuffled into the back room that served as kitchen and family parlor. Elizabeth led Lydia to a bench beside the open hearth and, once satisfied that she was in no danger of falling, took the long poker to stoke the near cold embers, blowing on the little red lumps of charcoal she uncovered. Once a small constant glow appeared, Elizabeth quickly added bits of kindling to create a steady blaze. Satisfied, she pulled three heavy logs from the rack beside the hearth and placed them into the fire. After checking that there was water in the iron kettle hanging above the flames, she turned back to Lydia.

"Child, ye have had an awful fright, but John is strong and can withstand much. Our task is to gather our wits and figure what is to be done to assure his quick release and safety. Such harsh times."

Lydia looked up at this woman, marveling at her matter-of-fact, take-charge manner. John's father was right. Mother Elizabeth was their rock.

Elizabeth placed her hand on her daughter-in-law's shoulder and gave it a firm squeeze. John's imprisonment was an unanticipated complication and placed the family in increasing danger. Elizabeth longed for the strength that her husband would have once provided, but admonished herself for such a futile thought. She knew that John ap Evan would give anything to be restored to his former self. He was such a good man. A spontaneous shudder wracked her body as she stared into the dancing flames. Taking a long, deep breath, Elizabeth shook her head and silently declared, No time for self-pity... *Thy will be done.* With John in prison, there was much to do, and it must be done quickly. She had to remain strong. Looking down at Lydia, she asked, "How are you feeling? Do you think you are ready for some porridge?"

There was a knock on the back door, and Elizabeth turned to see the huge hulk of their cottager's form fill the opening. "Owein, come in, come in. I've just put on the pot of porridge. You need much nourishment for all that must be done today."

A bent-shouldered man of middle-age shuffled into the room and placed a basket half-filled with brown speckled eggs on the kitchen table. Elizabeth motioned to a bench opposite where Lydia sat; he took off his hat, nodded, mumbled a thanks, and sat.

"Thank you, Owein, for gathering the eggs. Have the cows been milked, the horse let out to pasture?"

"Yeah, mum. I waited for Master John, but when I saw young Will Tatum at the door, I figured something were amiss and done what was needed on my own."

"That is good, Owein. How grateful we are for your dependable impulse. Master John was apprehended last eve for attending the gathering in the grove." Elizabeth placed a large bowl of steaming porridge on the table in front of Owein and motioned for the man to eat. She saw that Lydia had slipped out to fetch little Rebecca, who would be ready for her morning feed and was relieved that the young mother's strength had so quickly returned. Turning to Owein, who ate with relish from the steaming bowl, she continued, "Now the tending of the stock, plus reaping the rest of the hay must all be in your charge. Of course, Tom is here, but are either of your sons able to help? The first frost is but days away and there is so much to be done."

"Aye, mum. I can pull Idwal on the job, but we've not heard from Sior for three months past. His mum frets mightily on his whereabouts, as we've heard no words since

he headed north toward Chester." Owein put down his spoon
and drew his sleeve across his chin to indicate that he had
finished eating. "He's looking for a chance to apprentice a
trade. That restless lad finds the farm life not to his liking,
but I fear the openings be slim without family connection."

"How many years is your Sior now?"

"He be seventeen next spring. Never one to trouble his
ma, but she worries."

Elizabeth nodded, "Ah that seems to be a mother's
lot. I pray all is well with young Sior, such a good lad.
And Maryd?"

"Aye, yuh never see the wife without her needles, all the
day long knitting little sweaters and socks. She be mighty
lonesome with both of her daughters off married, more than
a day's trek from our shire, but their little ones, our five
grandbabes, will keep mighty warm this winter."

At that moment, the elder John limped into the kitchen
and sat down beside Owein. Elizabeth served him a bowl
of porridge before telling him of the previous night's events
and his son's imprisonment. As the older man listened, being
well familiar with the routines of Radnor jail, he sat quietly
for many minutes then asked, "Who is the night guard at the
jail these days?"

CHAPTER FIVE

October 4ᵗʰ 1681

"Noswaith dda, Master Vasser. I hope you are well this evening. The north wind begins to rise and it looks as if we might have frost before the morn." Lydia, wrapped in so many layers of wool shawls and skirts that she looked like a pregnant sow, stepped inside the heavy front door of Radnor jail and closed it behind her. "I've brought John some supper and wonder if you would be so kind as to let me see him, but for a moment. I promise not to tarry long."

She stood before a large, crumpled man in a filthy leather jerkin and coarse woolen pants, who sat behind a battered table in the drafty entrance hall of Radnor jail. Scratching the back of his neck and running his stubby fingers through the straggly grey hairs of a beard that merged with strands of dirty hair falling down his back, the jailor shook his head awake and looked at the round figure before him.

"Aw, Mistress Lydia, it must be frightfully cold outside.

You look as if you have every shawl you own atop your head."

Lydia hunched her shoulders and responded, "They say we might be in for a freeze tonight, so I must hurry to get home. May I go now to John?"

Benjamin Vasser, now fully awake, raised the napkin covering the large basket Lydia held, curious to survey the contents. He saw a round of cheese, fresh baked oat bread, a whole chicken turned to crispy perfection, some seed cake, and a small flask, probably some kind of home brew. "Your man sure won't go hungry tonight. He be luckier than those who have no family in these parts." Lydia reached into the pocket of her apron to extract two copper coins and held them out for Vasser while looking directly into the man's rummy eyes. "You know that he has not eaten in two days. You are so kind to let me pass."

She put the basket on the table and pulled off a chicken leg and pushed it into the jailor's paunchy hand, letting the succulent juices drip through her fingers. "This is for you, Master Vassar. I won't be long."

The man grunted, stuffed the chicken thigh into his mouth, and motioned Lydia on with a nod of his head. While still chewing, he gave a muffled stammer, "He's at the end of hall. Make it short."

Walking across the room behind Vasser, Lydia stood trembling on the top step giving her eyes a few moments to adjust before descending the dark, uneven steps leading to the dungeon below, afraid that her pounding heart might give way. The burning candle she held in her shaking hand barely illuminated the mat of cobwebs dangling from the low, rough-hewn ceiling beams at the bottom of the stairs. With courage she did not know she possessed, she tightened her grip on the large willow basket and stepped into the narrow passageway. As her hand brushed the wall, she instinctively jerked back, repulsed by the slime and mildew that covered the stones. Gripping her basket ever more tightly, she knew she must go down. John's life, their future, depended on it. The cellar was cold—not the piercing, bone-numbing blast of the near-gale-force wind she had struggled against on her trek to the jailhouse, but a dank, stolid, penetrating chill that engulfed her shivering body with the suffocating odor of animal decay and human refuse. Lydia gagged and swallowed hard in a desperate attempt not to loose the contents of her stomach.

Slowly moving forward on the dirt floor made hard by centuries of pounding feet, she came to a small area about six feet square and saw the hulky form of John's body lying on a pile of filthy straw, his face turned to the wall. A scrawny grey rat scrambled directly in front of her path. She quickly crossed the cell to stoop and touch John's cheek above the scraggly dark whiskers covering his lower jaw.

"John. John my love, I am here. I bring victuals." John spun over, flung his arms around her slender body, and buried his face in her bosom. He held her so tightly that she gasped for breath before nuzzling her nose into his tangled hair, littered with bits of dirty, sour-smelling straw. Lifting his head, John clasped his large fist around her shaking hand so that the half-burnt candle she held would not fall.

"Ah, Lydia, my sweet, don't set this wretched place on

fire. My current charge needs no amendment." He stood and pulled his young wife, who barely reached his shoulders when on tiptoe, to her feet to stand beside him. The shoulder seam of his waistcoat was torn, and the front of his once-white shirt, now splotched with mud, hung in tatters. She looked closely into his face to see that his left eye was swollen closed and a large, angry, purplish-red bruise splayed across his forehead.

Shocked, Lydia gave a shrill cry, "John, oh John, they've beaten you."

"Hush, little wife, our Lord will protect." Taking the basket from her, he lifted the napkin to examine the contents and said in soft, measured tones, "Ah, such a splendid feast… is the wine from the berries we gathered last summer?" Raising the basket to just under his nose, he inhaled deeply. "Fresh bread—surely just from the oven."

Lydia, marveling at his indomitable spirit, wondered how he could smell anything above the horrible stench of the prison.

"Eat quickly, John, while you listen to the plan."

Tearing a huge hunk from the loaf and covering it with a slice of Caerphilly he looked up. "Plan? What do you mean plan?"

"Hush now, eat and listen. There is little time. You see I wear many layers of clothing. They are your disguise for getting out of this wretched place. That old drunkard Benjamin Vasser is on guard above, and in about ten minutes, Owein comes to distract his attention. You, dressed in my garb, will slip by and out the door that Owein will leave ajar. Your mum is waiting in the wagon just at the corner. She will take you to Cardiff where you catch the boat that will take you to Amsterdam. All is arranged."

John flung the crust he was eating to the floor and grasped Lydia's shoulders giving her a harsh shake. "Have you lost your senses? I cannot. I will not leave you here. This is pure insanity."

Anticipating this very response, Lydia had rehearsed repeatedly for the past two days her next words. She knew that when John's pride was at stake, his convictions tested, his obstinacy closed like a forged metal trap. She had to lie. This was her only hope. Surely the Lord would forgive.

She looked defiantly up at her husband and said, "Vasser is in on this. He is only pretending to be distracted by Owein, as protection against Lord Manchet's wrath in case they might be observed. He will release me as soon as you are safely gone. Little Rebecca and I follow immediately. We will be on the next boat to join you in Amsterdam. There, the three of us," she silently considered if by that time it might be four, "will await your parents and the rest of the family. When the family is united, we will sail to Penn's Sylvania. All is arranged." She placed her small hand on his wrist, and with a firmness in her voice so that he could not mistake the meaning of her words, she said, "John, you put us all in great jeopardy if you do not follow this plan."

"Do you speak the truth?" Unblinkingly, John locked eyes with Lydia, and though she felt the muscle in her jaw twitch and the gorge in her stomach begin to rise, she held his gaze.

"Yes, John I speak the truth."

John, rebelling against the whole idea asked, "Why Mum instead of Tom to take me to Cardiff?"

Lydia responded quickly, "The gathering of the crops must be finished before the frost. Tom cannot be spared a day.

"How feeds our babe with you away?"

"Your sister Liz watches over Rebecca. Even if Rebecca refuses the milk-drenched rag, she will not go hungry. She now has begun to eat solids." Impatiently she stamped the sturdy leather boot she wore against the weather outside. "Hurry, John, we have not a moment to lose."

He continued to grip her shoulders as she unhooked the waistbands of her three heavy woolen skirts and let them drop to the ground around her feet. Standing in her light under-shift, Lydia said, "Make haste, John, I grow cold. Off with your trousers."

As he pulled her skirt over his hips, she heard the placket rip. "Here, John, I brought twine for you to wrap around your waist to hold the skirts in place. There are three, we can layer them around." When he was dressed, Lydia saw that her skirts barely reached mid-calf on his long legs.

Looking down at his crazy garb, he said, "You see, Lydia this is insane. It will never work."

Hoping her voice conveyed conviction, she said, "Oh John, you forget Vasser is in on this. Besides, he is half drunk and Owein is above to distract him. Bend low and move quickly." Eyeing her dubiously, John hesitated, but before he could offer more protest, Lydia reached up, brushed a kiss over his chin, and gave him a firm shove toward the stairs.

"Godspeed, my love. Be careful." Squatting low, John warily ascended the cellar steps, a paisley shawl over his head and a plaid tartan pulled tight around his stooped shoulders and over his face.

Owein dangled a large, limp hare in front of the seated guard, inviting Vasser's examination. "Yea, Vasser, I trapped him just minutes ago. Have ye ever seen such a fine specimen?"

Vasser poked at the inert, hairy body with covetous admiration, "Where?"

"The southeast corner of our field," Owein said, dropping the animal on the table as John shuffled across the stone floor behind the two men, inching slowly in an effort to be as inconspicuous as possible. As he reached the door, John had only to give a gentle push and it was open. He was through and standing in the cold night air.

Vasser momentarily raised his eyes to see the tail of a dark blue skirt pass over the threshold. "Good eve, Mistress Lydia, be careful," he called, before turning to stroke the dead hare and ask, "What did you use for bait?"

Elizabeth, hunched within a heavy blanket, was waiting in the wagon at the corner facing away from the church and the town square. John sprang up beside her as she flicked the reins and Cynwar launched into a swift trot down the narrow dirt road heading south. Mother and son did not speak. Their breaths hitting the frigid October air formed small white puffs as the two, concerned that they might be observed, silently scanned the darkness. The only sound was Cynwar's hoofs beating the soft turf, and, with no moon, the diamond-like glitter of the Milky Way seemed close enough to touch.

Back in the dank, dark cell, Lydia kicked the straw in hopes of scaring away any lurking varmints and sat down to wait, wondering what Vassar would do in the morn when he discovered he was holding the wrong person. What then? Nibbling on a hunk of bread, a precaution against intermittent nausea, she thought of John and his mother on their ride to Cardiff. How long would it be before she saw her husband again? She could hardly believe that he was gone. How could she face these next hours without him? It could be days, maybe weeks, even a month before she would see him again. Every muscle in Lydia's body was numb with exhaustion, yet her mind raced and she craved to hold her husband, to hold her baby, to be done with this ordeal.

She picked up John's torn jacket and spread it across the straw as she tied the napkin from the basket over her nose and mouth, hoping to block, or at least lessen, the terrible stench. Surrounded by prison squalor and dreadful darkness, Lydia had never in all of her life felt so alone. She struggled against the dark gloom seeking to engulf her heart and soul, searching for the beautiful light she had once seen in a dream so long ago. She was surprised. She had not thought of that dream, her friend Maryd, or her visit to Mabonig for years. How strange that memories from a time before she even knew John should come to her now.

"Mistress Lydia, what are you doing here? Where is

John? What…"

Jailor Vasser stood above her, the dim glow from his lantern barely illuminating his form, and though no morning light reached the cell, his presence meant the night was behind her. Her vigil was over. John should be in, or close to, Cardiff, maybe already crossing the channel. Sitting up abruptly, she was overcome with the agony of morning sickness, dry heaves, and dizziness.

"Oh, Master Vassar, where am I?" She looked around feigning confusion, then in a shaky voice asked, "Where is John?" Looking down at his trousers wrapped almost double around her waist, she said, "Oh, my goodness. Where are my clothes? Why am I wearing John's pants? What has happened? Where is John?"

Benjamin Vasser was a simple man, cruel to defenseless men and easily swayed by bribes of easy money, but he had a tender heart for this young woman. As a youth he had worked for Lydia's father, was treated decently, and fairly paid. He was totally confused at finding Lydia, instead of John, in his charge, and she was obviously hurt. It could mean only one thing. John Evans had overpowered his pretty, young wife, taken her clothes, and snuck past him in the middle of the night.

"What a low-down, good-for-nothing…Mistress Lydia, did he knock you down? Are you hurt? The stinkin rotter. I'll see that he pays for this."

"I'm not sure what happened. I wonder how he got away."

Stooping to lift and carry Lydia up out of the dismal darkness, Vasser continued to mumble to himself about the nefarious character of a man who would do this do his pretty, young wife. "I promise you, I'll capture John Evans before the day is out. Skin him alive. The scurrilous vermin, he can't have gotten far. We'll have the hounds out promptly."

Once above the cellar's stench, the fresh morning air revived Lydia and she begged off the jailor's solicitude to see her home. "Truly, kind friend, I am fine. It is but a short walk and you have your responsibilities here. The longer you wait to start the search, the colder the trail."

"Well, you be most likely right. I should get right onto finding that varmint. Are you sure you feel strong enough?"

"Oh, yes. Thank you. The day is fine and I'll enjoy the walk. And be assured that if John has the nerve to come near, or I hear of his whereabouts, you will be the first to know."

A light frost covered the ground but the brilliant blue sky with no clouds to the south lifted Lydia's spirits. The channel waters should be fairly calm for John, and Mother Elizabeth would have a good, clear day for her journey home. Turning to take the shortcut to their farm, the path across their neighbor's field, Lydia marveled at how easily she had lied to Benjamin Vasser; what's more, how easily she had lied to her beloved John. Surely, the Lord would forgive.

CHAPTER SIX

October 5th 1681

Benjamin Vasser trudged along the road leading to the earl's estate, knowing he would have to report John's escape to Parry ap Mullin, Lord Manchet's chief tenant. He dreaded the encounter.

Vasser had known Parry as a boy. Parry, fifteen years younger than Vasser, was the oldest son of the farmer who rented a large tract in the Wye Valley from Lord Manchet. Vasser always saw Parry as a cheeky lad, a nuisance to be around. But Parry obviously knew how to gain the earl's favor, while feathering his own nest, a talent Vasser never managed to acquire. Parry, now in his middle years, was married with six children and a large stone house. As a rich yeoman with substantial land holdings of his own, he also managed all of Lord Manchet's estate in the earl's absence, which was most of the time. The earl, like most landed gentry, spent at least ten months of the year in London or visiting the estates of other nobles and rarely appeared in Radnorshire, except during hunting season when he entertained large parties of red-coated huntsmen from all over Britain. Every autumn, wealthy aristocrats came in droves with their hounds and ladies to flush out the foxes, drink the cider, and feast in the earl's palatial hunting lodge built from stones gleaned from the ruins of the nearby eleventh-century castle.

Before mounting the wide slate steps to Parry's manor house door, Vasser took a flask from his pocket for a bit of personal fortification, reminding himself that he must address Parry as Mister Mullin. The highfalutin smugness that money gives a man was downright disgusting, but Vasser vowed to watch his speech. Show respect. It'd be terrible if John Evans' escape cost him his job. Night jailor was a heap better than slopping pigs.

The young girl who answered the door wore a white apron and maid's cap, but the heavy leather clogs on her feet and tangled mass of dirty brown curls springing out from under the cap suggested that she was new to the duty.

"Is Mister Mullin at home?"

"Yeah," nodded the girl.

"Ah, then I beg of you, please tell him Benjamin Vasser wants a word with him."

Without even a nod, the girl turned, left the door standing wide open, and disappeared. Vasser wondered if he should step inside the hall or remain on the porch. The brisk autumn air was chilly, and the hall, though unheated, would provide some warmth. Yet he figured it would be presumptuous for him to go into a house uninvited. Dithering, he stood shivering and waited.

"Benjamin, come in. What brings you out in the cold so early in the day? Don't tell me one of our prisoners has escaped." Parry Mullin, a barrel-chested, stocky man in his early forties with a full salt-and-pepper beard waved Vasser inside and shut the door behind him. "Let's go to the kitchen and see if Caitrin has a pot of tea on the hearth. Here, off with your coat."

Vasser let the other man help him with his coat. He decided to say nothing until they were settled by the kitchen fire. "Thank you, Mister Mullin. A spot of warmth would do me nicely."

Parry Mullin led Vasser down the wide hall past the hand-carved cherry dresser and stopped to remark on the collection of pottery on the upper shelves above the two drawers. "Here Benjamin, look at this Bartman jug. Some Frechen Stoneware that just arrived from Germany last week. What do you think? Is it the face of a Wildman or that of Cardinal Bellarmine?"

Vasser, in no mood for trivial games and having no idea what Parry was talking about, stopped to stare at the large brown water jug sitting on the shelf before him. A rather sinister bearded face imprinted on the side of the jug stared back at him. Parry, standing close to the other man's shoulder, said, "I'm really not sure. Some say it is the face of Bartman the Wildman who lives in the forest of the Rhine and protects the widows and orphans from marauding bandits. Others say that it is the spitting image of the Italian Cardinal Roberto Francesco Romolo Bellarmine, who was the arch enemy of the nascent Protestant movement on the Continent."

Vasser did not understand the question and knew not
how to respond, so he awkwardly shrugged his shoulders
and moved toward the open kitchen door.

The two men sat in comfortable armed chairs in front
of the kitchen hearth; the tea was strong and the fire warm.
"Now, Benjamin, what is your errand?" Parry asked.

"I hardly know where to start. A great travesty has been
done and an innocent woman maimed." Vasser, seeing he
had Parry's attention, continued. "Last eve, Lydia Evans,
such a pretty little thing, brought a basket of victuals to
John, her husband who had been arrested the day before."
The jailor paused to emphasize his next words. "One of
them nonconforming troublemakers. Well, anyway, she
begged to take the food to him…and me knowing her
since she was a small lass, saw no harm in that." Vasser
lowered his voice, wanting to swallow his next words,
"But this morn, when I went to check on the prisoner,
Lydia was sprawled on the straw in John's clothes and
John were gone."

"Wait a minute," Parry interrupted, "were you not at
your post the whole night?"

"Yes absolutely, on the Lord's honor. I even saw who I
thought were Mistress Lydia leave, wrapped all in her shawls."
Vasser shook his head and continued, "That scoundrel John
Evans knocked her down and stole her clothes, a disguise to
escape past me. The light were dim and I was havin' a little
chat with my friend, but I definitely saw who I thought were

Miss Lydia in her long blue skirt leave and thought no more of it."

"Hmm, so John Evans is gone. Have you called out the hounds?"

"Yes sir, since two hours past, but they've picked up no scent. It's as if John Evans vanished into thin air. Everyone within miles is alerted. When we find him, we'll haul him in, lock him up so tight, he'll never see light again," said Vasser, pounding his fist on the arm of the chair. "He'll be made to mind the king's law."

"How is Lydia?"

"Oh, she recovered fine...insisted on walking home by herself. So I could get right on the hunt."

Parry Mullin sat staring into the fire for several minutes, giving no indication of his thoughts. The worried jailor sat squirming and waited; Parry's next question surprised him.

"Who will manage John's farm? His father is broken and his brother, Tom isn't it? is too young."

"I dunno, I think Owein their cottager will stick with them, and the women are pretty strong."

"Many of those Quakers are selling out. Heading for America. Wonder if this might be on the Evans' minds," Parry mused. "I don't imagine we will see John Evans again in these parts. If that's the case, the family might be looking to sell and follow him." Parry looked hard at Vasser and said, "I want you to find out if the Evans plan to sell."

"Well, I might could listen round. Though I bet Mistress Lydia would never want to see that louse again, the way he treated her."

Parry stood up. "Benjamin, I want you to find out if the Evans plan to leave, but do not let on that I have any interest in the possible sale of their property." He set his empty cup on the table. "Well, time to go to work. Will you see yourself out?"

Relieved but puzzled by Parry's reaction, Vasser closed the front door behind him. He had not received even the slightest reprimand over a prisoner vanishing under his watch, without a trace. Nor did Parry seem at all upset that John took terrible advantage of his wife in order to escape. Parry hardly commented on Lydia's heinous mistreatment. On his walk back into town, the jailor struggled to understand why the earl put so much confidence in this man Parry ap Mullin.

A few days later, Benjamin Vasser saw Tom and Owein in the village talking with Baird Llewellyn, a neighboring farmer. Walking over to them, he heard Baird say, "Well, Tom, she is a healthy looking sow, but this ain't the time I'd normally be buying a pig, I've done my butchering for the year. She'd just be another mouth to feed through the winter."

"Yeah sure, Baird, but breed her after the first of the year and you'll have yourself a fine drift of swine by late spring. She's a good producer, never fails."

Walking up to the group, Vasser, asked, "What's up, Tom? Strange time of year to be selling stock."

Startled by the interruption, Tom looked up. Seeing who it was, he fought hard to keep a civil tongue, but knowing that rudeness would not benefit him or his family, he said, "Oh, hey, Vasser. Yeah, we are selling off. With John gone, we've decided to immigrate. Want to buy a pig?"

"Have you heard from John? Know where—"

Baird, interrupting, said, "So, that's why you're selling. Have any cows you need to get rid of?"

"Sure, and some of the best pasture in the area, plus twenty acres of tillable soil. Know anyone who would be interested?"

Vasser, without saying another word, turned and headed off to find Parry ap Mullin. He had heard all he needed to know.

Three days after her return from Radnorshire jail, Lydia was awakened in the middle of the night by severe cramps and a sticky ooze of blood running down between her thighs. Clamping her legs together and clutching her stomach, she let out a long, low moan, willing this not to happen. She rolled over, clinging to the sturdy post at the end of the bed to ease herself to the floor and crawl to a bag of clean rags in the corner. Her soul screamed in silence as she stanched the blood. Not yet two months in the womb, the nascent life within was gone. Sobbing, she prostrated herself on the hard, bare floor, with crashing waves of muffled sobs wracking her body. Finally, the night's chill set her teeth to chattering and she crawled back to the warmth of the bed John's parents had given to her and John as a wedding gift, four simply carved posts and a frame of walnut.

Her arms strained as she pulled herself up and under the covers to lie staring into the darkness, seeing nothing but feeling profound ambivalence. She felt terrible pain at the loss of a new child created by God and conceived through her deep love for John; yet, at the same time, though near impossible to admit, she felt undeniable relief that she was no longer pregnant. The birth and care of a newborn on the high seas would further complicate their already very difficult journey to America. She was thankful she had not shared her suspicion of pregnancy with anyone. Now, no one need know; yet this meant she had no one to share her grief. Her whole being ached for John. She had no word of where he was, or even if he made it safely to Holland.

Watching the moving shadow on the opposite wall cast by a bare branch of the giant elm outside her window tossing in the rising wind, she thought of the tales her grandmother told when she was a little girl, of the Little People's strange dance of death. Were they the ones who had taken her babe? The wind howled and the waning gibbous moon cast its eerie glow into her heart. Her longing for John felt unbearable.

CHAPTER SEVEN

Before the rural celebrations could commence on Nos Calan Gaeaf, *Winter's Eve, the cutting of the last corn, the storing of the harvest and the culling of the livestock must be done.*

October 31ˢᵗ 1681

"Morning, Sister Elizabeth."
"How are you, Brother Ian?"
"We've got a fine day for the task at hand. A cow, three pigs, and an old ewe. Is that right? 'Twill make a good morning's work."

Elizabeth opened the gate to the enclosed yard in front of the Evans' barn for Ian Jones to pull a heavy black pig by a rope around its neck past her into the pen. She closed the gate as Ian said, "Your black sow better have a tail. It's too close to Nos Calan Gaeaf to risk letting such a creature loose to wander the woods."

Elizabeth laughed wiping her hands on her apron, "Why, Ian, surely you don't believe that my sow would scare up a headless hag on the night of the roaming spirits? Besides, she will be bacon by then." Her neighbor chuckled and turned to speak to the elder John who limped out from the house to greet his neighbors and thank them for their help.

The crisp air and bright sunshine made for a perfect day for the task ahead. This was the day for folks from the neighboring households to help slaughter the Evans' stock chosen for their winter stores. Elizabeth, Lydia, Tom, Liz, Owein, and Idwal had worked sunup until sundown at the Addas' yesterday and two days before that at the Joneses. Neighbors always helped with the tasks where many hands were needed. Little Liz circled among the assemblage with a tray loaded with cups of steaming cider; the pungent scent of fermented apple mixed with the fumes arising from the hickory smoldering in the smokehouse filled the air. As the men in the group uncoiled their ropes and sharpened their knives, the heifer that had been chosen from the herd stood in its stall, contentedly munching her last meal.

Lydia volunteered to stay in the kitchen to oversee the potting of the meat, she dreaded witnessing fresh blood so soon after her recent ordeal. However, working in the kitchen kept her close to little Rebecca napping in her cradle by the hearth. Their neighbor, Isabel Llewelyn, Lydia's designated kitchen helper, leaned over the sleeping babe, observing, "What a lovely child—and growing so fast." A huge iron pot filled with water hung on the iron crane above the kitchen fire and a large red stone pipkin of melting butter stood at the corner of the hearth close to the heat.

An urgent pounding at the back door interrupted the women's chatter, and Lydia crossed the room to open it and saw Little Liz standing with an oaken bucket filled with the cow's innards and intestines in each hand. "Sorry, Lydia, kicking the door seemed the only way to catch your attention. These buckets are really heavy." Walking quickly into the warm kitchen, Little Liz set the buckets down by the chopping block and asked, "Do you need my help in here?"

Lydia thrust her hands into a bucket and lifted as much as she could hold onto the chopping block. "Thanks, Liz, I really think we only have room for two mincers at the block."

Lydia and Isabel set to chopping. The loud staccato beat of their pounding blades interrupted their chatter and Isabel's tale about her lost kitten. Half of the minced meat would be placed in the hot pipkin to bake in the butter, then drained and sealed with more butter. This delicacy could keep for more than a year, and Lydia wondered if some of this potted meat would be a farewell gift to friends who were helping them today. She doubted that it would travel well. The other half of the minced meat would be placed in the pot of boiling water with cinnamon, cloves, allspice, and sugar to simmer for hours. Some of this tasty preserve would surely accompany them on the high seas, along with the salted strips of beef that the others were hanging up to dry in the barn.

It was the last day of October exactly halfway between the Autumnal Equinox, September 20th, and the Winter Solstice, December 21st. Tom, Owein, Idwal, and two lads from the village, who welcomed the chance to earn six pence for a day's labor, had finished bundling the remnants of hay and oats from the fields and stood around the cutting box watching the season's forage being cut into winter feed for the animals. The chaff cutter, a stocky, muscular man dressed

in a long wool duster and matching knee breeches, was hard
at work. As an itinerant laborer, he traveled throughout the
shire plying his skill. Earlier that week he had promised Tom
that he would be sure to come to the Evans' place before
Nos Calan Gaeaf, the last day of October.

As the day drew closer, Tom worried, fearing the consequences to his family and their harvest, if the chaff cutter
did not come in time. Tom feared what the roaming spirits
of their ancestors, and no telling who else that appeared on
Winter's Eve, might do to those who failed to adhere to their
ancient traditions. Nos Calan Gaeaf, the night before the
first day of the darkest time of year, was a time when great
mystical powers were abroad. It was the one day in the year
that the veil between the world of the living and the world
of the dead was thinnest; all the laws of space and time were
suspended, allowing the spirits from the other world to walk
among the living.

Tom's fears were for naught. The chaff cutter kept his
word. He arrived at first light on that last day of harvest-time
and set up his portable mechanism, a three-legged pine box
with an open trough about nine inches deep, nine inches wide,
and three feet long leading to a scimitar-like curved blade with
a cranked wooden handle; a treadle beneath the box operated
a wood block clamp situated inside the trough just behind
the blade that would compress the straw before it was cut.
The two lads from the village, both no more than eleven
years, took turns filling the trough with hay. The chaff cutter,
using a short-handled fork, methodically embedded the fork's
tines into the hay in the trough and pushed it forward an inch

or so past the cutting edge of the blade. Then with his left foot on the treadle and his right hand holding the knife, he pressed the treadle down to compact the straw, raised the knife to a high position, and brought it down to slice the protruding straw into half-inch long pieces. This man was good. He worked in a steady, mechanical rhythm, making over fifteen cuts every minute. By mid-day Tom, Idwal, and Owein had covered the back wall of the barn with bushels of chaff stacked as high as a man could reach, the chaff cutter was gathering up his tools, and the young lads were skipping down the road with their hard-earned coins clutched tight in their fists. The Nos Calan Gaeaf deadline had been met. It was time to lay the bonfire.

The blazing flames shot high toward the star-studded sky, illuminating the faces of the entire Evans household and the neighbors who sat with them around the fire. Apples were roasting, walnuts were cracked, and cider poured round, while Owein, standing with his back to the fire, recited in his slow, rhythmic pace the ten verses of a traditional Celtic tribute to the spirits of nature and the departed ancestors of those who were gathered. At the conclusion of each stanza everyone chimed in to repeat the last line with Owein. When Owein sat down, the elder John stood, raised his cup, and said, "Honored ancestors! Old ones! Grandmothers, grandfathers, ancient heroes, elder wise ones, we listen for your wisdom. We thank you for allowing us to spend this time with you. We know the spirits will speak to those who will listen. Protect us now and let not the evil pranksters among you darken our door."

Everyone had inscribed his or her name on a flat white stone, and each in turn tossed the stone into the flames to mingle with the magic of the eve. Lydia had carefully written her name, Rebecca's name, and John's name on three separate stones. She knew that John, though not with his family on this hallowed night, would want the spirits of his ancestors to acknowledge him, wherever he might be. Rebecca, sitting in her mother's lap, reached for the dancing flames and Lydia hugging tight, nuzzled her cheek against the warm cheek of her babe, wondering if their ancestors would ever find them next year in the far off land across the seas?

Crunching on an apple, Tom turned to his sister who sat on a boulder next to him. "Hey Liz, I saved a pip for you." He carefully lifted a pip from his apple, squeezed it between his thumb and forefinger, and took careful aim.

Liz laughed, "Oh, Tom. There'll be no squeezing of the pips for me this year. My true love, if there be one, awaits my arrival on distance shores." Shadows from the roaring fire cavorted merrily on the two siblings as they bantered together, and Liz did not notice Idwal come up behind her, until he tugged at her sleeve.

"May I sit down?"

"Sure, Idwal, you know you don't have to ask. Why so formal?"

The cottager's son, a year older than Liz, smiled, settled himself cross-legged on the ground, and pulled a carefully wrapped bundle from beneath his jacket. "I have something for you."

Liz's eyes widened with anticipation and surprise. "Why,

Idwal, what in the world?"

The dark shadows hid the deep blush suffusing Idwal's face as he handed Liz the packet saying, "Liz, you will be leaving us soon. I've made something…" his voice cracked and his well rehearsed speech was abruptly cut short. He could say no more.

Liz carefully untied the string and folded back the wrapping paper. She held a large wooden spoon with a slender, intricately carved handle. "Oh, Idwal," she gasped, "this is beautiful."

"Liz, though you be halfway around the world, please don't forget us. I hope you like it."

Liz lifted the spoon up to the light by its shallow bowl and studied the long handle of oak leafs and flowers twined around a string of Celtic knots, topped by a winged Welsh dragon. Speechless, she ran her fingers over the silky smooth sycamore wood, letting her fingers, as well as her eyes, absorb the beauty.

"The dragon is for your protection…to always keep you safe."

Liz threw her arms around Idwal's neck, "Oh, Idwal, I love it. I've never seen anything so beautiful. I'll cherish it forever."

CHAPTER EIGHT

AN ORDINARY POSSIT: *Put a pint of good Milk to boil, as soon as it doth so, take it from the fire, to let the great heat of it cool a little; for doing so, the curd will be the tenderer, and the whole of a more uniform consistence. When it is prettily cooled, pour it into your pot, wherein is about two spoonfuls of Sack, and about four of Ale, with sufficient Sugar dissolved in them. So let it stand a while near the fire, till you eat it.*

—A Favorite Welsh Recipe, 1650

November 11ᵗʰ 1681

Without stopping to take off his milking boots, Tom rushed into the kitchen waving a large, folded piece of velum addressed in bold, black script. Breathlessly he shouted, "Lydia, Brother Aymes, just back from Amsterdam, brought a letter." A tall, gaunt man, dressed in a somber, black waistcoat and a wide-brimmed, black hat, stood stooped at the threshold behind the excited youth.

Lydia, alone in the kitchen stirring a fresh pot of possit, turned to grasp the letter and smiled at Jeremiah Aymes saying, "Come in, Brother Aymes."

But he quickly responded, "Mistress Lydia, I've traveled

the night through and am anxious see my own, so will beg off your kind invitation at this time. We will talk soon."

Lydia nodded. "You are incredibly kind to have come to us first. A true friend." Then, turning to her young brother-in-law, she said, "Brother Tom, you've surpassed Mercury in bringing me this message, but best not let your mother see the barnyard muck you've carried into her kitchen. Run now and fetch your parents for I know how anxious they are for news from John."

Before Tom was out the door, Lydia broke the letter's seal and began to read:

First Day of the Eleventh Month 1681

Dearest Lydia, My Most Beloved Wife,
Never before in my life have I felt such self-censure as when I left you to take my place in that foul prison. I trust that Vasser was good for his word and you were released within the hour. I marvel at your brave heart. It knows no equal. I am sure Mother related all there is to tell about the journey to Cardiff. Once I boarded the Christofer of Arnemuiden, *a rather small but sturdy vessel, it was less than an hour before we set sail. The sea was rough, and the waves gave us a good tossing, but the crew was competent and good company. Even though turbulent, the wind blew ever steady and we made it to harbor in Amsterdam in six days running. I slept much of the time and ate little, yet felt well rested on our arrival.*
The Society of Friends embrace me like a brother and I have already found work at the docks, but the activity of this

*city is beyond belief. Never before have I seen such a concen-
tration of people, work, wealth, and poverty in one place. It is
difficult for me to comprehend that there can be a spot on earth so
vastly different from our own dear Maesyfed. Though God's
grace has brought me here amongst such good people, city life
will not hold long, once the family is all together. The meadows
and farmlands of Penn's Sylvania are where we belong, for
there is where we will transplant our cherished roots in freedom.*

*With so many fortune seekers flocking to take advantage
of Amsterdam's robust commerce, housing is scarce. I lodge with
Brother Fassen's family. He is a baker, and my single room is
above the kitchen, so I wake each morning to the most delightful
aroma of freshly baking bread. I have many Friends looking
for more spacious lodging in anticipation of your and little
Rebecca's arrival. Yet, even if we have to share my one room
for a time, please, dear Lydia, come as soon as possible. Life
without you near is, at times, unbearable.*

*You must share with the others that since my arrival here
in Holland, my thinking has changed as to the timing of our
departure for America. You must tell the family that I have
become convinced that the sooner the entire family can make
it to Amsterdam, the better. Although I know we reckoned
eighteen months to wrap up all the details, I fear that every
day the family tarries under the stifling yoke of the King's men,
our situation grows worse. Selling our land quickly may, in
fact, bring us the best price. Those who have been in London
recently say that the King's lust for the high life and greed for
the spoils of war bring even higher taxes and depressed land
values. I am gathering the details of the cost and availability*

*for passage for the seven of us next spring and shall write
again soon.*

*My love and prayers are ever constant for you, dear Lydia,
and all of my beloved family. Come quickly. It is not good for
us to be apart.*

*In the name of and love for our benevolent Savior, Christ
Jesus, I am your ever-devoted husband,*

John

Several days after Lydia received John's letter, she crept
down to the kitchen very early to feed Rebecca before the
others were awake. Her spirits matched the dark storm clouds
gathering in the west. The grief, the loneliness, the longing
she feared she could no longer contain were ready to burst
forth. She needed to be alone. She could not let the others
sense her mood, see her tears. She did not want them, particularly Mother Elizabeth and John's father, to know of the
miscarriage, her loss, her apprehension about their future.
They had far too many worries of their own.

When John's little sister came into the kitchen, Lydia
said, "Good morning, Liz. I do hope you slept well."

Liz nodded, rubbing her eyes, said, "Lydia, you sure are
up early. Is everything all right?"

"I want to go make one last check of the garden to see
if any of the roots survived the frost. Do you mind watching
Rebecca for a spell?"

"Be gone as long as you like," Liz said reaching out for
the babe. "You know how I love playing with her now she's
crawling everywhere. Yesterday she pulled herself up on the

bench." Liz placed Rebecca on her knee, bouncing her up and down as the babe's fat, little hand reached out to grab a fistful of her aunt's red curls. "The way she is imitating sounds, it won't be long until she's making words."

"Isn't it wonderful to watch? Thanks again, Liz," Lydia said as she headed for the door. She intended to walk to the woods, try to connect with her grandfather's spirit, feel the presence of her Celtic ancestors, drink in the sanctity of the place that she would soon leave forever. She hoped to find some lost courage for all that she faced. But large drops of rain began to fall and she turned and ran for the barn.

Slipping inside the dark interior, blanketed by a heavy pungency of hay and horse, the light was barely enough for her to make her way to Cynwar's stall. Crossing her arms on the top rail, she let her head drop and felt the soft touch of the horse's muzzle nudge the hollow right below her ear. Owein, Idwal, and Tom had walked to the village. No one would come to the barn for hours. She was safe. She was alone.

Her knees buckled as she slid to the ground and sat not moving, staring into the darkness. Yes, John was safe in Amsterdam. But when would she see him again? Though she had promised to come as soon as possible, she knew she must stay here to help with the packing and the family's eventual transport. Duty, always duty, made her decisions, not the longing of her heart. But what were the longings of her heart, that heart that was being torn in two? She loved John, she was true to her vows, but to never see her mother, her father, her family, her land again…

Lydia's tears matched the heavy drops pounding on the

barn's roof, an unremitting torrent until at last they stopped. Having cried herself dry, she was exhausted. Her mind, washed clean, was still. Her heart was at rest. Lydia struggled to her feet, brushed her skirt, wiped her face with the corner of her apron, stroked Cynwar's neck, and returned to the house.

In late November, Parry ap Mullin came to the Evans' place for what he said was just a friendly visit—unusual, as no one could remember when Lord Manchet's chief tenet had ever before come calling. He inquired about their health, how they were getting along after young John's strange disappearance, and accepted a cup of tea before casually remarking that there were rumors about town that the Evans were considering immigration.

The elder John responded, "'Tis no rumor but the truth. We plan to sell out, lot, stock, and barrel." He blew a bit on the cup of tea in his good hand before taking a sip, then asked, "Interested? Tom and Sister Elizabeth will be agreeable to showing you around."

Parry ap Mullin walked over all of the Evans' land and inspected the house from top to bottom, inquiring on which pieces of furniture they planned to take and what would be the price of the items they were leaving behind. He spent several hours commenting that the house and barn both looked in good repair and the stock healthy.

A week later Elizabeth answered a knock at the front door to see a young farm lad standing in the cold. "Mistress Evan, I bring a message from Parry ap Mullin," he said in a mercurial voice, obviously going through the throws of change. Elizabeth took the vellum, read it quickly, and asked the lad to step inside while she penned her response. Parry ap Mullin had written asking her to meet him at her convenience at the New Radnor Inn across from the church the next day. She wondered if it was a ploy to keep her husband, a sharp business head, away from the negotiations. Why in the village and not at their house? She hastily wrote a note accepting Mullin's request, smiling to herself and secretly blessing this fortuitous development; Elizabeth knew that she was willing to lean on Parry's goodwill, even try to shame him a bit if he tried to take advantage of a cripple and his family, words that could never be spoken in her husband's presence. Before handing her response to the lad, she asked, "Would you have a cup of hot cider before you are off again?"

"Thank you much, kind lady, but Mister Mullin is most eager for your answer, so I best not tarry."

Elizabeth had agreed to be at the inn before eleven o'clock that morning; the walk to the village usually took less than three quarters of an hour, but she left their house shortly after the distant church bell chimed nine. Carrying the weight of the pending negotiation, she rehearsed again and again what she and her husband agreed would be the least they could accept for their entire holdings—tenant rights to their land, barn, stock, stored fodder, house, cottage, plus most of the furniture and household goods—wondering if Parry ap Mullin would drive a hard bargain. So much of their future rested on what transpired this morn.

Last night the elder John carefully advised what he thought was a fair price for each item and what was the absolute bottom price they should accept. As Elizabeth walked, she slowly turned the figures over and over in her head, the numbers jumbling together in a massive tangle. What would this day bring? Would she be able to hold her own? Perhaps she should have insisted that her husband accompany her today, or that Parry ap Mullin come to their house to meet with the both of them. Pulling her heavy wool cape firmly around her body, she gave her head a violent shake and asked God to lead her through the ordeal as she quickened her step toward the village.

It was late afternoon when Elizabeth, having been gone most of the day, came running into the kitchen waving a large sheet of vellum. Her face flushed not only from the bitter cold outside but from an excitement that drew the family's immediate attention; this was not Elizabeth their rock. Her normal, no-nonsense composure had taken leave.

The family had gathered around the kitchen hearth to await her arrival and all rushed to stand beside the elder John's chair to hear her news. Quickly untying the loose knot of strands under her chin, she cast her dark navy traveling bonnet on the kitchen table and shouted, "Look, look, every-one! Divine Providence works in our favor."

The elder John, sitting by the fire, reached out, "Perhaps you see the Lord's hand in your negotiations, Elizabeth, but I would like to take a look at the contract." With a triumphant smile, Elizabeth handed him the paper and he spent the rest of the afternoon carefully scrutinizing each detail of the proposal until he was satisfied that, though it might be providential, it was also fair.

The sale was consummated and passage was booked for the end of January on the *Christofer of Arnemuiden*, the same ship that had taken John across the channel. It was impossible to reckon exactly when they would leave; everything depended on wind and weather. All that remained for the family to do was pack. Each person was allowed one trunk for clothes, bed linens, and personal items; there would be one trunk for dishes and kitchen utensils and one trunk for garden tools and implements.

A few days before departure, Lydia and Liz sat on the floor amongst fragments of lavender, thyme, and rosemary, wrapping pewter plates and stoneware bowls with linen napkins to place with the pots and kitchen utensils in the open trunk that stood in the middle of the kitchen. As they worked they occasionally tossed a handful of the herbs into the trunk to sweeten the likely must of damp, salty air.

"Are you all packed?" Liz asked.

"Almost. I'm having a frightful time deciding if I can take the raspberry silk I wore at my wedding."

"Oh, you must. It's so lovely."

Lydia looked up at Liz, who, at fourteen, was already several inches taller than her sister-in-law and large-boned like her mother. "I wish you could wear it someday, but I doubt it would fit."

"I know you're right. I already tower over all of your family."

"And my shape has changed since Rebecca. I know I'll never wear it again…" Lydia sighed .

"You can save it for Rebecca."

Frowning, Lydia said, "No, at this point it would only take up precious space I need for more practical things. Besides, Mali, Haf, and Elian will be thrilled." Lydia sat back on her heels to reflect, "Kind of like a part of me will be able to be at their weddings." Rocking back and forth for a few moments, she picked up another bowl and laughed, "I guess it can be a new family tradition, a wedding dress of raspberry red."

CHAPTER NINE

January 15ᵗʰ 1682

The day before their departure, the Evans were to pay their farewell visit to Lydia's family. Looking out the window, Elizabeth exclaimed, "It has finally stopped raining. Why don't we walk over? If we stick to the path it won't be too slushy underfoot. Father you can ride Cynwar; he would enjoy the outing."

"Sounds like a splendid idea," the elder John said. "Tom, will you go saddle him up? I'm going to miss that old friend." When the family was ready to leave, Tom, helped his father into the saddle and stayed beside him as the procession walked across the dormant, winter, meadow scattered with patches of melting snow. As soon as they were in sight of the Cledwyn's house, Lydia's father, a short, wiry man with a balding pate, threw open the front door and shouted, "Welcome, welcome. We've been watching for you." All six of Lydia's brothers and sisters jostled out behind him, eager to usher their visitors into the stone-floored entrance and help them take off their wraps. Everyone was speaking at once as Lydia's mother, a short, plump woman in perpetual motion, bustled out of the kitchen carrying a covered platter and called, "Welcome, loves. Come, come along, you can do your visiting at the table. We don't want the food to get cold."

It was a tight squeeze, but all fourteen, with baby Rebecca on Lydia's lap, gathered around the large oak table piled high with bowls of roasted, winter vegetables, turnips, leeks, and beets. A platter bearing a leg of lamb surrounded by spiced, honeyed apples sat in front of Lydia's father's place. The small bottled-glass windows at the end of the modest hall let in the pure, fused light from the winter sun, and a mouth-watering medley of smells filled the room. Mister Cledwyn stood waiting until all were seated and the children relatively quiet before turning to his wife and asking, "Mother, may we begin?"

Smiling up at her husband, Mistress Cledwyn clasped her hands together, nodded, and bowed her head.

"Lord, we turn to you in gratitude for every person gathered at this table, and we ask a special blessing on John awaiting the arrival of his family in a distant port. We ask thee, Lord, to watch over us all, but particularly your brave children of the family Evans. Bless their journey and show them prosperity and happiness in their new land. Their leaving creates a great gap in the lives of us who remain, yet we rejoice in the knowledge that through thy mercy, we shall ever remain connected in love." Lydia's father's voice, assured and clear to this point, cracked on that last word. He paused and took a deep breath, indicating that he wanted to continue, then murmured a quiet, "Amen," followed by a low chorus of amens around the table.

The meat was carved, the vegetables passed, and the plates piled high. Lydia, who sat beside her mother, reached over and squeezed her hand. "Mother, this is a scrumptious feast. Thank you. I will certainly miss your cooking."

Twelve-year-old Barryn, swiping a lock of blond hair out of his eye, said, "I wonder what kind of food you'll get in America."

"Probably not much different from what we eat here… Once we get settled," said the elder John. "However, I'm afraid it will take us a few years to produce apples like these, so delicious."

With several murmurs of assent, the families continued eating, but the mood became increasingly somber. Even Lydia's fun-loving siblings, normally a noisy, boisterous lot, were tongue-tied with the enormity of the occasion. Mistress Cledwyn, closely monitoring everyone's plate, provided most of the conversation. "John ap Evan, you must have another helping of lamb. Lydia, I baked those apples especially for you—do have another. Now, everyone, please eat up…but save room for the Bara Brith and butter pudding."

As he took the last bite of pudding, Mister Cledwyn raised his glass, "Daughter, our love for thee travels wherever you land. Know that we will pray daily. You are with good folk." He turned to nod and look directly into the eyes of the elder John, Elizabeth, Tom, and Little Liz. He then rose, pushed his chair away from the table, and went to stand beside his daughter. Removing a small leather pouch from his vest pocket, he placed it on the table beside her. "Your mother and I are by no means wealthy, but we want you to have this. Put this in your sock for a time when you might need it."

Lydia, handing Rebecca to her sister Elian, who was sitting beside her, jumped up and threw her arms around her father and held him tight. Then, turning, she knelt beside her mother and buried her face in the generous lap that had been her refuge since infancy. Her mother quietly patted the top of Lydia's house bonnet. No words were spoken.

Very early the next morning, with all of the farewells to family and friends having been said, the Evans family began the first leg of their long journey. The farm wagon, loaded with their trunks and boxes, stood ready for departure as Lydia stepped across the worn threshold of the Evans' house for the last time. Pausing to soak in the beauty of her beloved Maeysfed, she gazed out over her cherished land. The heavy, pre-dawn mist covering the hills seemed like the tears of untold generations, bidding a lachrymose and final adieu. Lydia handed Rebecca up for Liz to hold, as she climbed atop the trunks alongside Tom and his sister. Beneath the dangling feet of their children, the elder John and Elizabeth sat on the driver's bench beside Owein, who would take them to Cardiff and return the wagon and Cynwar to their new owner.

CHAPTER TEN

January 21ˢᵗ 1682

J ohn, tired from a long day at the docks, entered the smoke-
filled tavern and was relieved to spot a small, vacant table
in the far corner against the wall. Stopping by the crowded bar, he picked up a tankard of ale and ordered a bowl of
house chowder and a slab of cheese before elbowing his way
across the room. The cacophony of German, French, Italian,
Swedish, and Polish, plus languages he did not recognize,
created an isolating din for which he was thankful. With no
energy or inclination to socialize, he sat silently sipping his beer,
observing fellow refugees, other newly arrived immigrants
drawn to Amsterdam by its tolerant liberality and burgeoning commercial prosperity.

The past weeks had been hard. Although at the first of the
year he found better pay in the shipyards plying his carpen-
try skills rather than loading cargo, the dreary weather and
continual rain fostered a moroseness he assiduously prayed

to avoid. But, tonight he was unable to escape the doldrums. His unceasing longing for Lydia, his anxiety for his family's safety, his self-recrimination for not sharing in the monumental tasks surrounding their departure from Maeysfed, as well as loneliness, fear, and guilt weighed heavily on his soul. Knowing that, according to the latest letter, the family should arrive in less than a week, his mood darkened as he visualized their perilous channel crossing in rough, winter weather.

"Ist das Stühl frie?"

John looked up to see a tall, stooped-shouldered young man with hollow cheeks and a tentative expression standing before him. Though resenting the intrusion on his solitude, John, realizing the young man would probably not understand Welsh, responded with an inborn sense of hospitality in halting English, "No, no, please sit down."

"Ah, Sie kommt von England...I know but a little of your language."

"And I know none of yours. Parlez-vous Francais?"

"Nien, no. Nür Deutsch and a bit of English."

The German lowered himself into the chair opposite John as the barmaid appeared with soup, bread, and cheese. Setting it down before John, she asked the newcomer if he wished to order anything to eat.

"Nien, danke. Nür ein Bier, bitte."

Eating the hearty, surprisingly tasty soup, John's natural conviviality began to return and, seeing that his seemingly distraught table-companion might welcome a friendly word, and hoping his rudimentary English, so different from his native Welsh tongue, would be understood, he asked,

"What brings you to Amsterdam?"

"I study art with masters. Rembrandt allows me into his studio."

Although John knew little of art, he had heard of this artist from some of the artisans in the Society who occasionally had a commission from a wealthy tradesman or one of the aristocracy in the city. "Ah, you sit at the foot of a great man. You are fortunate."

"Bestimmt…indeed, but I have much to learn. And the tutelage does not come cheap. The price of paint and canvas inflates by the week."

John wondered if this was the reason the young man ordered no meal. "Come, have some bread and cheese, they brought far more than I can eat." The younger man at first hesitated, but then shyly nodded acceptance and murmured his thanks.

John asked, "Have you been in Amsterdam long?"

"But three months, yet, now I must leave, but…" his words trailed off as he bowed his head and stared down into the tankard of beer the barmaid set before him.

Not wanting to pry, but sensing the young man wanted to say more, John asked, "Troubles?"

Close to tears the other responded, "I just now, today, received word that mine Mutter, mother, is very bad ill. I have no money for travel. I could seek work at the docks. Two weeks wage might be enough…but…"

"I know the docks and have a contact that might take you on. The pay is good for the man who works hard," John offered.

"Yah, two weeks wage might be enough…but by then she might be dead."

"Where are you from?"

"A small hamlet on the outskirts of Munich. I can work hard, but I fear any delay." The young man looked searchingly into John's face, drew in a long deep breath and said, "But, I might have other possibility. Think you I could find a man who would buy this?" He hesitantly reached inside his shirt under the frayed collar and pulled out a small leather pouch. Unknotting the strings, his long, paint-stained fingers withdrew a lovely brooch, the color of sunshine, and placed it on the table between them.

John stared at the sparkling gem surrounded by tiny seed pearls. "What a lovely piece."

"Ist wahr…very true…it has amazing charms. The old woman who lives in the lodging where I have my room told me of the topaz's special qualities."

John, mesmerized by the beauty of the gem, asked, "What did she say?"

In slow, stuttering speech, carefully measuring each word for a meaningful translation, the young artist said, "Well… according to ancient wisdom…she said the brilliance of the topaz helps he who wears it absorb Gött…God's light. It helps the wearer bring in from the universe, from God, what is needed. It allows he who wears the topaz…to…surrender to the pre-planned destiny that is set up in the beginning."

John felt a jolt of recognition at the young man's words. This gem was meant for his Lydia. Had she not already absorbed God's light? How else could she have found the courage, the strength to take his place in prison so that he and their whole family could escape to freedom? Was it pre-ordained? Did not the topaz symbolize Lydia's absorption of the inner light, her personal courage, her ability to listen and trust in God's plan?

"What is the cost of the fast coach to Munich?" asked John.

"The coachman said he would take me for six florin."

John, who had carefully husbanded every copper stuiver that had come into his possession since his arrival in Amsterdam, pulled out his money pouch and counted out eight silver florin. "Here, my good man. I will have your golden topaz and you shall kiss your mother's brow before the end of the week. Make haste."

The young man's dark blue eyes stared in disbelief as his words stumbled over one another, tears of gratitude rolling down his cheeks, "Danke schön...thank you...Viele Dank... Danke, Danke, Danke...mein herrlicher Mann."

John picked up the topaz, placed it in its pouch, and, after putting the precious gem in his inner vest pocket close to his heart, he stood, grasped the young man's narrow shoulders with his large, rough hands and pulled him to his feet saying, "Godspeed, my young friend. May Christ's blessings ride with you."

CHAPTER ELEVEN

January 26ᵗʰ 1682

"Master Evans, Master Evans, she's here...just rounded the point and is but a half hour from dockside." Nine-year-old Jeremy, son of another Quaker émigré, true to his word had stood watch for John every day during the past week to alert him the instant he caught sight of the *Christofer of Arnemuiden*. After confirming with the man with a telescope who stood next to him on the pier that this was truly the right ship, Jeremy covered the two hundred yards to the carpenter shop in record time. Now panting, proud to be the bearer of the good news, he beamed as he watched John strip off his leather apron and grab his jacket and hat.

Then with unbounded glee, Jeremy felt himself lifted onto John's broad shoulders, like a royal prince on a spirited steed far above the heads of the pedestrians below. He grasped a lock of John's long hair to maintain balance and they set off for the dock. Jeremy's short legs would have in no way matched John's Goliath strides as they rushed down the muddy thoroughfare, dodging carts and slow-paced idlers, to meet the incoming ship. For the first time in weeks, the rain had stopped and the sky was a deep cerulean blue. After so many dark, dismal days, the bright sunshine dazzled their eyes.

There they were—Lydia, Rebecca, Father, Mother, Tom, Little Liz—all on deck, all leaning far out over the rail, straining to catch sight of him, amidst the magnificence of the buildings and wonders of this huge, bustling port that claimed to be the center of world. Tom was the first to spot John; waving frantically, he touched Lydia's arm and pointed, obviously shouting, but still too distant to be heard.

The next half hour, as the ship maneuvered into shore, seemed an eternity, but then the gangplank was lowered and Lydia, holding little Rebecca (much grown in the past four months), was beside John, engulfed in his embrace. Now with the family reunited, he knew the Lord's blessings were upon them; they would know freedom—freedom of action, freedom of worship, freedom of conscience, freedom to build for generations to come. All these glorious freedoms awaited them in America, thanks be to God.

The family, with all their belongings in tow, was carted to their temporary lodging in an inn two blocks from the wharf. Over a dozen Friends from the local Society were waiting, eager to welcome the Evans to Amsterdam. Introductions were made all around and pleasantries exchanged. Brother Fassen presented a basket of fresh bread, preserves, and pickled herring to Elizabeth and gestured to all the family saying, "John has won our hearts since his arrival in our city; how he has pined for this day. We all continually prayed for your safe arrival and bless the Lord you are finally here. I know you are worn thin after such a long journey, so we now take our leave for this night. Please know we are here to offer whatever assistance we can as you prepare for your ocean voyage."

The family gathered around a corner table in the inn's dining area and, over a hearty meal, John ap Evan told his son the details of their property settlement, noting, "The Lord smiles on our venture. We have money enough for transportation for the whole family and the purchase of two forty-acre plots of land in Penn's Sylvania, one for you and Lydia and one for Tom."

After dinner Little Liz asked, "Can Rebecca sleep with me tonight? I would so appreciate her company in the new, strange place."

Lydia readily agreed, "Of course, dear, she would love your comfort." Even though bone-tired, Lydia silently rejoiced, her heart skipping a beat, knowing that this first night together after so many months, she would have John all to herself. Elizabeth, seeing the elder John fighting to hold his eyes open, stood to bid goodnight to the others and excused herself, leading her husband up the stairs to their assigned bed chamber. The rest of the family soon followed.

When they were at last alone in a small room, barely larger than a broom closet, John quietly closed the door, took Lydia's two hands, and gently led her to the bed. "Lydia, please sit down, I have something for you."

She lowered herself to the edge of the bed and looked up, smiling in anticipation. "John dear, no gift could be better than being again with you." She patted the quilted counterpane, "Please, sit beside me."

John, reaching into his pocket, pulled out the small leather pouch, "Lydia, my love, this topaz is meant for you. A wise old crone who saw this brooch revealed an ancient truth. She said that she who wears the topaz absorbs God's light...she knows and acts on God's pre-planned destiny." John paused, lifted one of Lydia's small hands from her lap and placed the luminescent brooch in her open palm. "Lydia, my love, the inner light shines forth from you. You are meant to wear the topaz."

At first Lydia was speechless. Then, with a slight, teasing smile, she held the brilliant little gem before the candle's flame and murmured, "So many facets." She gave the small gem a slight swing so that it cast beams in all directions.

"We know the source of the light, but where do all the beams lead?

Oh John, I pray that we, our children, and our children's children always stay connected to the source. It is lovely, John, thank you."

CHAPTER TWELVE

Ancient Britons who boasted no Anglo-Saxon blood, claimed genealogies traceable to Adam. Thomas John Evan, who arrived in the Province in April 1682, four months before the larger migration, was typical of most in first learning to speak and read English tolerably well on the long voyage across the Atlantic.

—The recollections of David Lloyd, 1740

April 1ˢᵗ 1682

"**L**and a Ho!" The cry from above, like a voice from heaven, instantly charged those below into furious activity. Half clad men, women, and children scrambled from their bedrolls, threw on any excuse for an outer garment, and swarmed onto the upper deck. The elder John approached his daughter-in-law saying, "Go now, Lydia. Leave the babe sleeping. I'll climb the ladder later, after the crush."

The young mother hesitated. How oft her father-in-law was penalized because of his injury, but Mother Elizabeth gave her a slight push, "Come now, dear, we've prayed over many months for this moment."

Lydia placed a swift kiss on the elder John's brow. "Oh, thank you Father, you are a saint." She grabbed John's hand

and rushed up the ladder topside with the others.

The early morning fog was lifting and the sun, low in the eastern sky, shot dancing rays of salmon pink across the steel grey surface of the water. Far in the distance, Lydia saw a long, low lump of dark on the horizon.

"That must be Cape Mey, named for the Dutchmen who first landed here," John exclaimed. "It's our entrance to Delaware Bay."

"Oh, John! John, we are here." Her arms flew around his waist and he pulled her close to his side as the two stood, leaning against the rail, watching the dark mass of the peninsula that protected the waters beyond take shape. A steady southeasterly wind nudged the *Godspeed* past the point and they entered the wide estuary outlet of the Delaware River. They would know landfall in Penn's Sylvania by day's end. As they looked out over the marshy shoreline a huge flock of white geese rose hundreds of feet in the air, and as if in salute, welcoming them to their new homeland, the birds turned in a single wave and headed inland.

Spotting Rufus, one of the younger passengers, up on the quarterdeck, John left Lydia's side and climbed the steps to join him. The young man was talking with some of the crew and did not see him coming. John tapped him on the shoulder and pulled him aside, saying, "Rufus Sweete, I have waited to talk with you until this day. Now, thank the Lord we are here."

Rufus smiled and said, "'Tis a new day in a new world."

John smiled and continued, "Lydia and I are in need of extra hands as we establish our homestead and would like to pay for your passage in exchange for four years of your labor. You will have to work hard, but you will be fed well."

A broad grin spread across Rufus' freckled face as he grasped John's hand. "Ah, John, my prayers have been answered. You will not be sorry."

By mid-afternoon Lydia, holding Rebecca's hand, lost her balance walking up the uneven path strewn with small, sharp stones. John grabbed her elbow to keep her from falling and chuckled, "It will take a while for you to regain your land legs."

The small band of weary passengers off the *Godspeed* slowly worked their way up to the grassy knoll at the top of the hill where Brother Lloyd stood looking out over the rolling fields of tender green spotted with indigo-dark woods. The air was fresh but gentle; a most welcome change from their life for the past eight weeks in cramped, inhospitable quarters. None of the passengers had private cabins. The middle deck where they prepared meals, ate, and slept was divided into open stalls, like a horse barn. In spite of rough weather, they would climb up on deck as frequently as possible to gulp in fresh air and gain relief from the dank, dark, suffocating stench surrounding their coffin-like spaces below.

Yet, in spite of the insufferable conditions, with little difference between day and night, Lydia rarely heard any complaints from her fellow passengers. Ancient ballads and hymns were sung, family memories shared, and a particular rock or wooded stream in their beloved homeland described.

When there was sufficient light, those who could read, read aloud to the others from their Bibles, but candles to provide light below were permitted only when the sea was close to dead calm.

The large barrels of fresh water lashed to the bulkheads on the main and quarterdecks were for drinking only. Seawater had to be used for laundry, and Lydia soon found that dried salt in little Rebecca's diapers against her tender skin created an itchy rash and a miserable baby. Rebecca remained bare-bottomed for most of the voyage. But today they had arrived, and Lydia could hardly wait to wash their garments, rank with two months of wear, in fresh, clear water.

Brother Lloyd, with raised hands, was speaking, and many of the bedraggled passengers dropped to their knees. Lloyd's voice was soft, his words distinct. "Brothers and sisters, the Lord is good. He watched over us, we forty souls who ventured forth from our familiar homeland to forge a new beginning. Our benevolent Father has brought us to our journey's end in this beautiful, verdant land. With grateful hearts, we rejoice and give thanks. We are blessed. Yet, with our words of thanksgiving, we must pause to give a special prayer for Brother George and Sister Elizabeth Gates, who bid final farewell to their infant son, baby George, taken on the high seas to his permanent rest with our Lord." There was a perceptible nodding of heads, but no one else spoke. Now off the *Godspeed*, everyone felt profound relief. Smallpox had invaded a sister ship a month before and twenty-three souls on that ill-fated voyage were buried at sea.

Wagons driven by grubby looking men speaking a strange language pulled up next to the landing where the cargo was being unloaded. Wooden crates, large and small trunks, and bulging hemp sacks, stained black from weeks in the ship's hole were piled high on the wharf. A well-dressed man in knee britches, worsted waistcoat, and tri-corned hat, obviously the proprietor's agent, stepped forward with a large, official-looking sheet of parchment.

In the distance on the edge of a clearing underneath a stand of giant elms, stood a cluster of curious natives. Glancing in their direction, Lydia felt a deep blush and automatically lowered her eyes. The men were stark naked, except for small cloths across their loins, elaborate strings of beads around their necks, and brightly colored feathers fixed in their thick, black hair. She knew that Brother Penn had gone to great lengths to befriend these natives and she also knew that they were purported to be a most helpful, friendly folk. Yet, she had never seen so much bare skin on any man, except, of course, her husband, but then only in the privacy of their bedchamber. John, noticing her agitation, gave another chuckle. The relaxed mirth in his voice, like a chorus of chirping tree frogs, was a sound she had not heard since months before he left Maeysfed. Lydia's heart continued to sing in silent thanksgiving.

She turned to her young sister-in-law and asked, "Liz, could you watch after Rebecca for a spell? I want to help your parents supervise the unloading of our goods."

John walked up to the man with the parchment and said, "Good day. I presume you are Brother Penn's agent. My name is John Evans. Both my brother, Thomas, and I put in a request for forty acres each in the Welsh Tract."

"William Markham is my name," said the elegantly dressed man. "Yes, I am Penn's agent and his cousin. Do you have papers?" Scrutinizing his parchment, he continued, "I see your names at the top of our list. I can ride out sometime tomorrow for you to select your plots. Today I must stay dockside to supervise the unloading of the vessel."

John turned away and pulled out the large leather purse containing all their legal documents and money that he kept hidden beneath his shirt. He handed Markham the evidence of their claims for land in the Welsh Tract west of the Schuylkill and said, "I also wish to purchase the passage for Rufus Sweete, one of the indentured passengers."

John met Rufus, a firm-muscled lad of sixteen from Lanycil, one afternoon during the first week of transit, when he and Thomas, propped against some water barrels up on the quarter deck, were drilling each other on English declensions. They noticed the youth standing a few feet away listening intently as they tried to master the new language. Tom, called to him, "Hey there, it's a language we all got to learn. Want to join us?" Rufus eagerly accepted and the three young men studied together, a couple of hours every day, for the remainder of the voyage.

The Evans family agreed while still in Amsterdam that on reaching Penn's Sylvania, Thomas and John would each take forty acres in the Welsh Tract. Both of the brothers wanted their parents to live with them; their mother's practical good sense and their father's near saintly faith were an asset to any household. However, it was decided that the elder John, Elizabeth, and Little Liz would live with Thomas. Although Thomas hoped he would find a bride before the year was out, his homestead would need womanly skills for the kitchen and household chores from the beginning. Even when he met a young woman to his liking, and she felt the same impulse for him, it would take months for the Society to investigate a potential wife's worthiness before permission to wed would be granted.

And too, John and Lydia, anticipating that other children would soon be joining Rebecca, were eager to establish their own place. Since there was little money beyond the amount needed for the land purchase, only one day laborer would be hired, and he would stay with John and Lydia. These practical decisions were easily made on the sure knowledge that the foundational rock of their new life was a benevolent God and their Quaker community. All the brethren and sisters in the Society would help each other in the major work of establishing and sustaining a place in their new land.

When John, who planned to contract an indentured on their arrival, realized Rufus was looking for a master, he discussed purchasing Rufus' passage with Lydia. She eagerly agreed. She liked the quick wit of the young towhead, who reminded her of her young brother Barryn.

By the middle of May, with weather warming and days lengthening, the family left their lodging at the Boar's Head Inn close by the harbor and moved to a large lean-to constructed of bark and stripped birch branches on their property. They had spent every day since their arrival clearing, tilling, and planting their land in preparation for next year's harvest. Men from the Lenne Lenape village up the river helped the Evans construct their provisional housing, and, though it was not as substantial as the natives' permanent houses, it was made from the same materials. Lydia had lost her initial shock at the natives' lack of proper clothing and enjoyed watching the playfulness they brought to their work. More serious labor was taking place a short distance up the creek. John and Tom had hired a crew of scruffy Swedes, who had settled in these parts years before, to help them build a log house on each of their allotments. Working ten, sometimes twelve, hours a day, the family would have solid roofs overhead by mid-summer.

One morning after the men folk departed for their construction sites, Elizabeth and Lydia leisurely chatted over their second cup of tea, watching a mother robin build her nest among the branches of a giant elm that stood next to the clearing. Little Liz and Rebecca had wandered into the nearby woods to gather dry twigs and branches for kindling. On finishing her tea, Elizabeth picked up the large, grey hare that lay at her feet. Stepping to a rough plank balanced on two sawed-off stumps, she took a long-bladed knife and swiftly skinned and gutted the animal. Wiping her hands on her smudged apron, she sat down and said, "Glad John's trap worked. This one will make a tasty supper. But, I do miss my stone oven. Guess I'll have to sit and turn a spit most of the morning."

"It is a shame our big pipkin broke in transit, ah well, we will have our hearth ovens before the..." Lydia stopped in mid-sentence as she saw a statuesque Lenne Lenape Indian woman with a slight limp approach. Their visitor was carrying a large, beautifully decorated clay pot. Elizabeth and Lydia stood as the woman stepped before them and extended her arms in a gift-giving gesture. Her gentle, dark brown eyes looked directly down into surprised and somewhat apprehensive hazel eyes.

As Lydia gathered her wits, she nodded, took the pot, set it on the ground, and gestured for the woman to sit on one of the logs by the fire pit. The woman gave a slight smile and made a few unintelligible sing-song sounds, but instead of sitting, she turned and pushed several of the stones at the edge of the pit into the center to form a type of platform in the middle of the embers. In a deferential, yet, self-assured manner, she surveyed the campsite and, spotting a basket of carrots and leeks, took several of the vegetables, dipped them into the bucket of water that Lydia had fetched earlier that morning, and gave them a thorough scrub.

Elizabeth and Lydia stood silently and watched as their mysterious visitor placed the vegetables in the pot. She then turned to Elizabeth and indicated that she would like the cleaned hare, which she gently dropped in the pot on top of the vegetables. She again looked around and touched her finger to her tongue and shook her fist over the pot. Lydia, interpreting her sign language, went into the lean-to for their saltbox and held it out for the woman. After a sprinkle of salt from the box, the Indian visitor picked up the pot and placed it on the newly constructed stone platform in the middle of the pit. With a long stick she carefully pushed the live embers around the base of the pot before piling big stones around and over the smoldering fire.

Grasping the Indian woman's hand, Lydia exclaimed, "Mother Elizabeth, you don't have to sit by the fire all morning. Our new friend brought you a Lenne Lenape oven. It's beautiful. Thank you. Thank you." But it was not words but the gestures and smiles of the two Welsh women that conveyed their gratitude, and the Lenne Lenape women nodded and walked back into the forest.

Preparing meals on an open campfire; learning to cook in the Lenne Lenape pot, washing their clothes, herself, and little Rebecca in the icy cold creek, and sleeping under the stars were new and exciting. When an occasional downpour drove the family under their temporary lean-to that kept them surprisingly dry, the scent of the damp bark, reminded Lydia of the beloved wood sprites she thought she had lost forever. Her new life was taking on its own strange and satisfying rhythm. By mid-August the two log houses were finished. Lydia, John, Rebecca, and Rufus moved into one of the new houses and Tom, Elizabeth, the elder John, and Liz set up housekeeping in an identical structure a quarter of a mile down the road. The following year, the Evans' combined eighty acres produced a fine harvest and their grain sales were robust.

Philadelphia's port boomed with trade. Items both practical and extravagant were flowing in from all parts of the world—glass windows and wares, tools, machinery, porcelain, earthenware, silver, pewter, herb and vegetable seeds, English furniture, Turkish carpets, fine linen, silk, lace, calico, and woolen goods. The trade with colonists on Caribbean plantations was especially vigorous. The islands in the West Indies grew plenty of sugar used for cooking, making molasses, and distilling rum, and Caribbean settlers needed Pennsylvania wheat and pork. Yet, one type of cargo repulsed Lydia and the entire Quaker community—the ships arriving from Africa and the Caribbean with human beings for sale. The Society of Friends had issued a formal protest against slavery, but their ban was not effective in stopping the trade.

William Penn's tolerant policies encouraged settlers and traders from all around the world. Farmers, artisans, merchants, seamen from any faith or no faith came. Everyone was welcome, even pirates and brigands, as long as they did not disturb the peace. For those who did break a law or became a public nuisance, a large locked cage stood in the middle of High Street, a block from the wharfs, where miscreants were placed on public view. What bothered Lydia the most were the bands of jeering children who threw rotten fruit and the mocking adults who hurled equally disgusting taunts at the prisoners.

In the spring of that following year Lydia had another miscarriage, and despite John's urgings, she insisted that he drive their cart alone to Saturday market. Dreading the bustling crowds of strangers in all manner of dress on the crowded, noisy streets filled with filth, she always found a chore at home that needed immediate attention.

June 1685

"Father, please…please let me go." Four-year-old Rebecca was standing in the yard begging. Her grandmother, Elizabeth, had taken Rebecca with her when she rode to market with John a few weeks before.

"Please, Father, please."

"I'm sorry, Becky. I'll be too busy to take you around town, and sitting in one place all day get's mighty boring for a little girl."

Rebecca pleaded, "Can't Grandma go?"

"No, child, not today. She has to tend to your grandfather who's been running a fever for over a week."

Lydia, who earlier that morning refused to even consider taking Rebecca to market, now watched her daughter and realized that she must overcome her reluctance, her fears. Philadelphia and market days were an important part of their life. Yes, there were evils in the city, but there were also many intriguing, instructive and fun things to do.

From that day forward on Saturdays when the weather was pleasant she and Rebecca always rode into town with John to enjoy the rich display of wares, buy a taste of licorice, laugh together at the gaudy dress of the seamen, and listen to the macaronic blend of foreign tongues. But as they wandered through the maze of stalls and down side streets into inviting shops, Lydia assiduously avoided the corner on High Street where a prisoner might be caged and the wharf area where they would come within earshot of the auctioneer's call at the slave block.

September 1686

Five-year-old Rebecca, wearing her First Day best, a blue calico dress trimmed with narrow strands of crocheted lace, sat squirming on the braided rug covering the floor of her parents' bed chamber as she watched her mother pin her long hair into a tight bun at the nape of her neck. Lydia turned to her daughter and said, "Please, dear, be still for just a moment more. I'm almost ready. You mustn't get dirty before we leave for Meeting." After lifting her best bonnet off of its stand and tying its ribbons securely under her chin, Lydia picked up the brooch from her dressing table. But before pinning it to her dress, she slipped down to sit beside her daughter, asking, "Rebecca, do you know what this is?"

The child's fingers reached out to stroke the smooth stone. "I love the way it feels," Rebecca said. "Didn't Father give it to you a long time ago?"

"Yes, dear, your father was put in prison in Maeysfed because he believes we all should be able to worship God freely. That is why I always wear the brooch to Meeting." Lydia held the topaz up to the morning sun coming through the window. "See how it reflects God's light?"

"Grandma told me that Grandpa also went to prison."

"Yes, Grandfather John, God rest his soul, was a saintly man who suffered much for his convictions. I wish he had lived longer so you would have known him better. I have never known a stronger, yet gentler man. We all miss his wisdom."

"After his funeral, Grandma said that even though we buried him in the ground, his heart is always with us."

"Your grandmother speaks the truth. Come now, we mustn't tarry a moment longer. Your father is waiting for us outside."

CHAPTER THIRTEEN

January 1689

L ydia knew that the number seven held magical power but was not sure what it might mean for her life. The ancients had named the days in the weeks for the seven planets in the heavens to symbolize the cyclical nature of the cosmos. Even though the Society of Friends did not accept such pagan designations, she wondered at their significance. Did the number seven symbolize the cyclical nature of the lives they lived below on earth? They had lived in their new land for seven years and so much had changed. Wondering what their next seven years would bring, Lydia stood at the window, still weak but grateful to be at last standing after weeks of convalescence.

The world beyond was completely white, save for the brilliant blue of the sky above and the dark shape of the log house on the next ridge, where Rufus and Molly now lived as cottagers with their two little ones. Two years before, when limestone was discovered in the Schuylkill River bed, she and John decided to build a replica of John's childhood home in Maeysfed—the two-story, stone, foursquare with a slate roof. Through frugal and careful management over the seven years since their arrival, John and Lydia had not only been able to buy more land, they were able to build this Welsh-style house where they now lived.

Lydia, John, and Rebecca had moved to their new home the previous September in plenty of time before the baby's anticipated arrival in December. John was worried. Over the past four years Lydia had suffered three miscarriages, so he insisted that, this time, she must get extra help. Rufus' young wife, Molly, a charming young Irish girl full of spunk, was willing, but with a fifteen-month-old toddler and three-month-old baby, hardly able.

A few weeks before their move, Lydia and John had walked across from their log house after supper to inspect the oak sapling John had planted that morning. Sitting on the porch of their nearly completed home and enjoying the radiant rays of brilliant orange and lavender flooding the evening sky, Lydia asked, "Do you think Leke Natap, little Natap's mother, would be interested? She has such a lovely spirit. Though we still hardly understand one word the other says, we are in complete communion. Remember the huge clay pot I cooked in that first summer? It was Leke Natap who gave it to me."

Lydia thought back on her first meeting with this tall, slender, brown-skin woman with a slight limp, high cheekbones, and luminous eyes from the Delaware tribe. Though awed by the Lenape woman's height, a full head taller than she, and her regal bearing, Lydia felt the warmth of her friendship from the very beginning. "Rebecca and I met her and little Natap while we were gathering berries last week. The four of us sat for hours on the riverbank, tossing pebbles, eating berries, just being together. It was lovely."

John smiled, "It won't hurt to ask. I know Mother will want to help with what she can, but she's moving mighty slow these days—our stairs would give her a problem."

Lydia nodded, "And too, she'll be needed at Tom's with Mary expecting their fourth in February. I wouldn't be surprised if it's twins. She already looks bigger than I, and I have only two months more."

John stood and extended a hand to pull Lydia up beside him. "I'll ride up to the village tomorrow. If Nooch is there, he can translate for us. I believe I'll take Becky along. She might help in the negotiations. I'm sure if Leke Natap is willing to help, she will bring little Natap."

Lydia exclaimed, "Oh, Rebecca would be thrilled. I've been planning to start her reading lessons once the cold weather sets in, and I could teach the two together."

Leke Natap and her little daughter did come. Lydia wondered if she would have survived last month without Leke Natap's practiced knowledge and obvious experience of child birth; her calm, soothing assurance when things went wrong. The baby, a little boy, was delivered stillborn after hours, upon hours, of hard labor. The midwife from the

Evans' Quaker congregation, who was expected to oversee the delivery, was with fever in her own bed, unable to assist. Although other women Friends from the Society came, it was Leke Natap who quietly assumed the critical role. Leke Natap knew how to stanch the bleeding and calm the completely exhausted Lydia. And over the following weeks it was Leke Natap who tended to Lydia's every need, washing her every morning, feeding her corn soup and nursing her back to health while managing the household and the two little girls with remarkable ease and good humor.

"I'm pleased to see you up," John said entering the room, his ears and nose red from the freezing outside temperature. He walked up behind Lydia and wrapped her in his arms, kissing the top of her head, noticing the first strands of gray intermingled in the curls of chestnut brown. Hesitating, not wanting to share the news Rufus brought earlier in the day, yet, knowing that waiting would not make it easier, he said, "You must not get chilled, my love. Come back to bed and we will talk." He pulled the quilt up over her gaunt figure and sat down beside her on the edge of the high four-posted bed.

Taking her small hand in his large, rough palm, he said, "Lydia, dear, you must be clairvoyant...Mary birthed twin boys this morning." John felt her fingers tense and saw her eyes snap shut as she drew in a shallow breath. He said nothing as he watched one large tear slide down her cheek. She withdrew her hand, swiped the moisture away, and opened her eyes.

"What a blessing. How is everyone doing?"

"Fine, as far as I know. Rufus came over a few minutes ago, a long trudge through the snow, to give us the news.

Lydia, gulped hard, trying to hold in her words without success. "John, are we cursed? Is the Lord punishing us? Am I not worthy? Tom and Mary are now blessed with five young souls. We came to this new land to give our children a better life. Yet, where are those children?" Lydia's voice caught in her throat. "Thank God we have Rebecca." Sobbing, she crumpled into his outstretched arms and he let her sorrow flow.

"I so want her to have brothers and sisters...for you to have a son."

Holding the woman he cherished above all else in the world, John said, "Lydia, love, you are my family, I would be lost without you. We are in a dark time now, but the Lord is with us. We must have faith."

April 1689

On a warm morn with jonquils popping up around the edge of her kitchen garden and a fat robin tugging at a worm in the dark, recently turned soil, Lydia began to feel the light returning. Rebecca was lying on her back in a patch of grass telling her mother about the huge dragon in the clouds above. Lydia called to her, "Come, little one, let's pick a bouquet to take to Aunt Mary and visit your new little cousins." Rebecca sprang to her feet and ran with pigtails flying, to catch her mother's hand.

"But first, come inside. I think you are old enough now

to know more about my topaz brooch." The two climbed the stairs and entered the master bedchamber at the head of the landing. Crossing to the dressing table on the opposite side of the room, Lydia lifted the lid of a handsome rosewood box and took out the small leather pouch. Turning to Rebecca, she kneeled down and patted the floor beside her, "Come Becky dear, sit down.

"You've many times heard the story of how I fooled the silly jailor in Radnor when your papa was in prison, so he could escape to Holland. And when I finally was able to join him in Amsterdam, he gave me this beautiful brooch. You've seen it many times. It is my most prized possession."

"I love the way it sparkles."

"Yes, dear. And it is now time for you to know what the topaz symbolizes. For one day, Rebecca Evans, this brooch will be yours." Holding the gem up to the light, Lydia said, "See how the topaz, the color of our jonquils, catches the sun and reflects our Lord's light? The Lord's light within our hearts is precious, the most important thing in our lives." Putting her arms around her daughter and giving her a tight hug, Lydia continued, "This topaz symbolizes that light to me. I hope with our new beginning in our new land, our family never looses it."

CHAPTER FOURTEEN

L ydia moved the spinning to the back stoop hoping to catch some breeze. Instead, a blanket of thick, still air intensified the oppression of the stultifying heat. Worried about Rebecca, who complained of a stomachache earlier that morning, she asked, "Feeling any better?"

Small droplets of perspiration covered Rebecca's fourteen-year-old brow, and the normal sparkle of her bright blue eyes was changed to a dusky, opaque film. "Mama, my tummy really hurts. I'm afraid I might vomit."

"Come, dear, though it is horribly hot inside, at least you will be out of the sun. You need to lie down." Lydia made a soft palette in the dark corner of the parlor away from the windows and lifted the sweat-drenched shift over Rebecca's head before she told her to lie down.

"Dandelion tea will soothe your stomach. I have a jar cooling in the creek."

Reaching the small stream located about twenty yards from the house, Lydia met John coming in from the field.

"I've taken the cows into the woods again today. I hope they can find some fodder there. This drought has turned our fields to stubble. We are in serious trouble. If it doesn't rain soon, we could loose our animals as well as our crop."

Lydia, focused on her immediate concern, seemed not to hear his words but registered the sound of his voice. "John, you are here." Wringing out a rag wet with stream water, she handed it to her husband. "Becky is feverish. This should cool her brow. I'll be along with some tea for her stomach in a moment."

When Lydia reentered the house, John was on his knees holding Rebecca close to his chest. Her limp body was shaking violently. Instantly beside her daughter, Lydia held her head in one hand and raised the cup of cool tea to her blistered lips. But Rebecca did not drink. With a near violent thrust, John passed his daughter into her mother's arms and rose abruptly.

"I'm off for the doctor. Dear God, please let him be home."

Philadelphia was an hour's ride on a swift horse. Dr. Graven's house, a new, two-and-a-half-story brick, sat in regal isolation in the center of a recently surveyed city block on the western outskirts of town. He was one of the four trained physicians in the region's burgeoning population of over four thousand souls. The doctor had moved to this section of the city to be closer to his Quaker brethren, mostly farmers in the Welsh sections near Chester and New Castle. However,

Dr. Graven's tender care and reputation for vigilant inquiry into the origins as well as the treatment of disease brought many Swede and Finnish patients from the older part of town down by the docks. Occasionally a harlot, who lived in one of the caves in the high cliffs above the river, needed his care. Dr. Graven went willingly; he never refused. But once assured that his patient was on the mend, he would admonish her in gentle but firm words on the moral degradation of her current occupation.

"Surely, my dear, you will know a better and more joyous existence if you but learn the Lord's ways."

Though his care was cherished, his words rarely had effect.

Lifting the heavy brass knocker, John pounded, impatient for a response. When the door opened, he was relieved to see Dr. Graven standing before him, blinking and a bit disheveled from being aroused from his afternoon nap.

"Brother Graven, it's my daughter, Rebecca. She lies abed with fever, very ill. Can you come? Now."

The doctor stepped aside. "Come in, John. Fetch a cool drink from the pitcher there on the sideboard. The wife is at the millinery…the governor's ball is next week. I'll grab my bag of tools and write her a note, then we'll be on our way."

John stepped into the darkened vestibule, past the doctor, and through the door into the dining room. He saw a covered pewter pitcher on the sideboard and quickly poured himself a tall tumbler of water, draining it down in one long draught.

Leaving the house, the two men entered the shed and Dr. Graven said, "Bet you want to wipe your steed's flank while I harness and saddle mine. Here's a curry brush. There's water in the trough…don't let him take too much too fast." John appreciated the unhurried but efficient attention to detail his friend displayed. It would be another hard ride, another hour, before they could reach Rebecca.

As the scorching mid-day sun subsided into the longer shadows of late afternoon, Lydia moved Rebecca onto a mound of grass in the shade of the tall oak tree to the east of the house. The soft, almost imperceptible rustle of the broad leaves above seemed to quiet the girl's tremors, but the heat of her body continued to escalate. As Lydia tenderly swabbed her daughter's burning brow, she noticed a slight rigidness in Rebecca's limbs—was this just a projection of her own mounting tension and fear? Her tears mingled with her sweat, *"Oh, dear Lord, be with us. Take away this malady that consumes our Rebecca…Dear Lord, be with us, oh dear Lord, be with us now…"*

"Lydia, may I please examine Rebecca?" Lydia looked up to see Dr. Graven and John standing looking down. She had not heard them come up and wondered how much time had passed since John set out with such urgency. Lydia relaxed her embrace and lay the inert youth flat on the palette at the doctor's feet. John held out his hand to assist his wife as she stood and leaned against his stalwart form. The doctor bent down and began his examination.

He gently pried open each eyelid to inspect the lusterless clouds beneath. He then opened the mouth, sniffing the girl's shallow breath. Taking a wooden swab from his black satchel, he scraped over the gray, mushroom-like tongue. Next, he lightly probed and punched her entire torso, probing thoroughly around her stomach and lower abdomen. The girl did not stir. She gave no indication that she felt a thing.

Lydia blurted, "How could such probing not awaken her?"

Dr. Graven stood and took a large, freshly laundered handkerchief from his trouser pocket. Slowly wiping his hands, he raised sad eyes to meet Lydia's anxious gaze. "She is not sleeping, Sister Lydia. Rebecca has slipped into a coma."

A sharp intake of breath preceded a low, barely audible wail as Lydia dove to scoop her daughter into her arms. Sitting on her haunches, she swayed back and forth, rocking in rhythm with her sobs. "Do something, Doctor. You must do something."

John visibly shaken asked, "What do you think this is?"

Dr. Graven responded, "I fear it's Milksick. I have never actually seen a case of this dreaded disease, but have read about the symptoms and the cause. My understanding is that if a cow eats an herb called snakeroot, I am not certain if it is found in our local woods, it will poison the cow's milk. The ingestion of such milk is lethal in most cases. There is no known antidote."

John could not believe the doctor's words. His heart raced, he heard ringing in his ears, his vision blurred, his eyes sprung closed as crashing cymbals filled his brain. Nothing, nothing in his life had ever struck so hard. He could withstand prison, beatings, hardship, poverty, failure. But not this. Had he murdered his daughter? *Oh God, thou hast forsaken me.*

"Could there be snakeroot in the woods? What have I done? The cattle had no fodder. I let them graze in the nearby woods. Oh, God."

Graven saw the impact of his possible diagnosis and grasped his strong hands around his friend's shoulders to lead him away from his wife and daughter. "John this is not certain, we will search the woods and run more tests. But, in any case, you must not blame yourself."

Tearing at the roots of his hair, John's sobs echoed those of his wife as he stumbled forward, only able to walk because of the doctor's firm support. Dr. Graven, almost certain what further investigation would show, knew that this man and this woman would need an immeasurable amount of consistent support from everyone in the Society in the coming years. Rebecca's life slipped away within the hour.

Late October 1695

A gathering of five women sat quietly in the Evans' parlor. Ever since the day after the funeral, three or four Quaker sisters appeared at least twice a week to sit with Lydia in the afternoon, to share her grief and pray with and for her. The women usually brought handwork, embroidery or knitting; they always brought quiet sympathy and wisdom. Those in the Society believed that no one should suffer alone. They believed that only through open sharing would Lydia regain her connection to life and to God. Time, patience, and prayer.

As one of the women got up to add a log to the fire she remarked, "I feel a bit of a chill. They say we are in for a hard freeze tonight."

The young matron sitting beside Lydia observed, "I guess the Indian Summer on First Day this week was our last touch of warmth for the year."

The others murmured assent and Sister Lloyd said, "Yes, it was good not to have to light the braziers during worship. The sun's warmth after Meeting felt so good." Turning to Lydia she said, "David remarked that he certainly appreciated talking with John."

Lydia looked up. There were dark circles under her eyes; her skin reflected the sallowness of her soul. "Oh really? John and I rarely find anything to talk about these days." She quickly dropped her eyes and stared at her small bony hands clasped in her lap. What was there to say?

September 1696

John stood looking down at the small stone marking his daughter's grave, staring at the indelible date. It was over a year since they buried her. The light that had ignited his life was extinguished. His daily routines continued—he tended his crops and livestock, he provided for Lydia and Rufus and his family, he contributed his labor and resources to his community—but it was as if a heavy sack, tied tight at the neck, covered his head. All about was dim and lifeless. Sometimes he found it hard to breathe. Yet, he worked. He worked hard, harder than he ever before had worked, and his fields, trice doubled since their original purchase of four-teen years before, were producing crops this year that would yield top price. Why should last year's drought that led to the loss of his only daughter, his only child, be followed by this perfect growing season?

Lydia and he no longer shared the commodious bed-chamber at the top of the stairs. He now slept on the narrow daybed in the study below on the ground floor. Yet, life continued. Every First Day the two went to Meeting together and dutifully visited his mother and Tom's growing family. Lydia washed and mended his clothes, tended the garden, and prepared their meals that were eaten in silence. Still, at the beginning of each meal, as if by rote, they faithfully bowed their heads and he offered a brief blessing. There seemed to be no relief for this pair of brooding, broken hearts.

With the farm's increased earnings John bought land on river's edge and built a gristmill to grind his and his neigh-bors' grain. He ground the harvest, as sorrow and desolation ground his very being. More work was all John knew to do.

April 1697

Dr. Graven and his wife, snug in their parlor on a rainy afternoon, lingered over their First Day evening ritual: a small glass of Madeira before their light supper on the cook's night out. "Charles, I am terribly concerned. It has been nearly two years since little Rebecca's passing, yet Lydia and John's spirits remain dead to each other. It is like standing barefoot in a frigid snow bank to be with the two of them together."

"I have tried to talk with John, tried to convince him that he bears no blame, that one cannot be held accountable for what one does not know; but like Job, he rebuffs my every overture."

His wife nodded and said, "If only they could see what they are doing to each other. Strange how sorrow creates a selfishness that builds a wall around one's heart." Standing to walk to the window, she observed, "The rain seems to be letting up. We should take a walk, see if there's a rainbow."

"Do you think Lydia blames John?" the doctor asked.

"Oh no, I don't think so," his wife quickly responded, "Yet, it is hard to know what she thinks, she has so little to say when we women gather. But there seems to be no blame, only sorrow."

"Uhm, the longer they withdraw from each other, the more it becomes habitual," the doctor mused. "Yet, now that spring is here, I pray their hearts will begin to thaw."

A few miles away, Lydia, seeing the rain slacken, decided to search for mushrooms while there was still light. She stepped outside with the door standing open behind her and was nearly blinded by the rays of the sun, low on the horizon, illuminating the water droplets clinging to the spring-green leaves and grass; the woods looked like they were on fire. Awestruck, she paused to drink in the beauty and noticed a doe and her two fawns in the middle of the distant meadow. This was too lovely not to share. Without thinking she called, "John, come look."

He approached shyly, cautiously, and they stood quietly

beside each other for several minutes until the three deer bounded off. Without saying a word, Lydia picked up her mushroom basket and stepped out into the glow. John followed. For the first time in almost two years, Lydia and John went to the woods together.

As they approached the creek, she heard a mockingbird overhead and, looking up, missed her step, lost her balance, and sprawled into a mud puddle headfirst. John was beside her instantly. "Lydia, are you all right?

She sat up, feeling muck between her fingers but no pain. With a short laugh, she said, "I think all that is hurt is my self-esteem." Her face and bonnet, as well as her clothes, were covered with a dark, oozy slime. John pulled a kerchief from his pocket and gently tried to wipe some of the mud from her cheek. He paused and looked into her eyes.

"Lydia, I've missed you."

"I've missed you too, John.

In late afternoon of the Eleventh Month, on November 1, 1700, at the farmstead of Lydia and John Evans in Chester County, Pennsylvania, another John Evans was born. Over the next twenty years, nurtured and loved by his adoring parents, he grew into a capable and handsome young man.

PART TWO

JANE

CHAPTER FIFTEEN

May 1721

"Mother, did you notice the new family at Meeting this morning?" Jay's hazel eyes, shaded by the broad brim of a black felt hat, revealed an unusual spark as the young man turned to the older woman seated beside him. "Do you know who they are? I've not seen them before. They were sitting near the back of the hall and did not join in the Conversation."

Lydia and her son were riding in the small cariole John had purchased three years before. She had protested mildly over such untoward extravagance, yet he insisted that they could well afford it with wheat sales at a premium and, what was more, he had said, "I want the family to have a proper conveyance when dressed in their First Day Go-to-Meeting clothes." Now on this lovely May morning, bouncing home over the rutted dirt road, she had to admit that the thick leather-covered horsehair upholstery was far more comfortable than the wooden plank seats of their utility wagon.

Lydia and her son, John, whom the family called Jay, were returning to their farm on the outskirts of Chester after the Society of Friend's First Day Meeting in Haverford. Her husband, John, had to stay after the service to meet with the other elders. The Lenne Lenape, the friendly tribe the English speakers called the Delaware Tribe, were concerned over changing interpretations of the original land agreement that William Penn had made with their people in 1682. John told his wife and son not to wait for him. He would catch a ride with their neighbor, David Lloyd.

On such a glorious day, mother and son could not help but enjoy the brilliant freshness of new spring. The steady beat of horse hoofs on the hard road, the slow easy rock of the cariole, the pungency of freshly plowed earth, the distant chirp of robins building nests among the branches of the giant elms all promoted an easy, near languid conviviality. Lydia felt bemused satisfaction as she thought of the two most important men in her life, her two Johns. To an outsider the continuation of one name, John Evans, from father to son and on to grandson, with no numeric designation or middle name distinctions, probably created confusion; but the continuity pleased her. Jay, the young Pennsylvania John Evans sitting beside her, evoked strong memories of the proud, handsome Welshman she had married over forty years before.

As she turned to look at her son, Lydia sensed that his question indicated an inner stirring that did not match his assumed casualness. She smiled at the strong, handsome profile of young Jay Evans, now in his twenty-first year, her only surviving child, and responded to his query. "The family arrived in Philadelphia about two months ago. Thomas Howell is, I believe, a baker from Bristol, a port city not very far from where your father and I grew up. I met his wife, Phoebe, at our women's gathering last Thursday. They have three children. Their eldest, the lass who caught your eye, is Jane." Lydia watched a red blush suffuse her son's neck and cheeks as he stared straight ahead.

Taking off her bonnet and turning her face to the warm, welcome rays of the midday sun, Lydia closed her eyes and touched the smooth stone encased in tiny seed pearls pinned to her bodice just below the hollow of her still slender neck. She let her fingers trace the small, even facets around its edge, and wondered if Jane Howell might be the woman who would someday wear her topaz brooch.

CHAPTER SIXTEEN

Late May 1721

Two weeks later folks in the Brotherhood were exchanging pleasantries outside the Meetinghouse after an unusually long service when Jay spotted the Howell family across the lawn and asked, "Mother, there are the Howells, will you introduce me?"

Lydia smiled saying, "Why of course, Jay, come along." She led him over to where Phoebe and Jane Howell stood waiting for Brother Howell and his two sons to fetch their wagon.

"Sister Phoebe, I'm so pleased your family is joining our Conversation and wanted you and your Jane to meet my Jay." Jane's green eyes danced under arching dark brows, the same color as the long curls that billowed from beneath her bonnet.

Jay, obviously uncomfortable, stared at a spot five feet over and beyond her left shoulder and stammered, "Sister Howell, my mother says you come from Bristol."

Muffling her amusement at his shy awkwardness, Jane

extended her hand, knowing that Jay Evans would never match the easy charm of a previous beau; yet, she found the wide brow and even features of this tall, quiet man surprisingly attractive. Jane, unusually tall for a woman, looked directly into his face and said, "Why yes, Jay, we do come from Bristol. I spoke with your mother last week. She indicated that we might have mutual interests."

At that moment, a large officious looking woman with a huge bonnet covering her dull grey hair walked up and said, "Sister Lydia, could I have a word with you? It's about the Barton matter."

Lydia excused herself, saying, "Sister Phoebe, Jane, I look forward to seeing you again soon. Jay, I'll wait at the carriage for you and your father. He said he would only be a few minutes."

She walked off with the older woman who was holding her by the elbow and bending close to her ear. Jane's mother smiled saying, "I think I'll go see if I can find your father."

Alone with this beautiful girl, Jay felt lost and was unable to meet her eyes. Looking down at his feet, he gathered his courage and asked, "Sister Jane, would you entertain my calling on you sometime?"

"That would be very nice," she quietly answered. "Would you like to accompany me to the Meeting next Wednesday evening?"

He looked up quickly and answered, "I would indeed."

She saw that his eyes were hazel like his mother's and smiled, "Thank you, Jay. Why not come a few minutes before seven? Do you know where I live?"

He liked the sound of her voice, low and lilting. He was entranced by the greenness of her eyes, the soft glow of her complexion, the fact that she stood only a few inches shorter than he. Wednesday evening seemed years away.

After that Wednesday and over the following months, Jay appeared on Jane's doorstep almost every evening as soon as he finished his late afternoon chores. During those long summer twilights, the two young folk strolled along the river, stopping at a bend or on a bridge to try to glimpse a trout flitting amongst the rocks. Jane enjoyed Jay; he was good company. In unbounded enthusiasm for the land, he made a game out of his desire to teach her all about her new country. On their walks he would pluck a leaf from a branch asking, "Now, Sister Jane, what kind of tree is this? I told you last week." Or, after a summer shower he would say, "I bet I can find more mushrooms than you."

Having grown up on the busy streets of Bristol and helping in her father's bakery, Jane had always viewed the woods a nice backdrop for occasional excursions—a pleasant change from the stimulating bustle of town living. Jay challenged her to learn about the wonders of nature, to look carefully and appreciate the details of what he called "God's bountiful beauty."

One Saturday around dusk, as they stood at the river's edge leaning over a clear deep pool, Jane said, "Jay, let's try our luck at catching a fish for dinner tomorrow. Since it's a First Day and you won't be working the fields, we could come right after Meeting."

"What an idea," Jay responded enthusiastically. He marveled at the easy camaraderie he and Jane were establishing. Not having a sister, he knew little about the daily routines or interests of girls his age, and Jane's keenness for outdoor adventure surprised him. Even more surprising was her obvious interest in the business of the farm, an activity from which Quaker women were traditionally excluded. Jane's natural curiosity as to how it all worked did not offend, but only added to her allure.

On a market day in mid-July, she rode with him into Philadelphia and rather than browse the shops and stroll the park, which he expected her to do, Jane insisted on staying by Jay's side during all his bargaining, bartering, and sales. On the way home she peppered him with questions. "Jay, how do you decide the price you will ask? Do you lower the price if someone buys more than one basket of beans? You said your father wants to purchase some more acres and will have to ask for credit. How does he figure how much he can borrow?"

Jay himself was just learning the answers to such questions, and it helped him to better understand what he knew and what he did not know when he and Jane talked about the business aspects of farming that his father was teaching him. The more he was with Jane, the more he knew he wanted to be with her always. But he did not know how to put his desire into words. He let her do most of the talking and enjoyed hearing her stories about growing up in Bristol—her family's annual trip to London, their large apartment above her father's bake shop, and the friends she left behind. However, there was one story Jane did not share with Jay.

Although she felt a growing affection for Jay, Jane wondered if she would ever again feel the same compelling passion she had felt for James Reardon. Even now her memory of him quickened her heart—those meaningful glances that made her feel she was the only person in the room, the light graze of his fingers against her shoulder that sent a tremor up her spine, flattering whispers that she was the most beautiful woman in the world. She could still hear his words, "Jane, my beauty, my life would be nothing, mere dust, without you. You must be with me forever."

A week before the Howells were to sail for America, she was ready to confront her parents. The family was finishing their evening meal, and she waited for her brothers to scrape the last morsel of pudding from their bowls and leave the table before stating in well rehearsed, measured words, "I have decided that I am not going to America. I can't go. I am going to marry James Reardon."

Her words hung suspended. No one spoke until her normally mild-mannered father stood, grasped her shoulders with hands made strong by kneading dough, and pulled her up to stand before him. In a voice she never before had heard, he asked, "Daughter, have you lost your senses? You will not marry such an unworthy man. I know of his devious practice...his deceitful ways. His character is rotten. You surely know that any man of merit who wants your hand in marriage would come in person to ask my permission. Yet, I well understand his lack of propriety. He most certainly knows what my response would be. That man would ruin your life.

You would be disowned by our Society. He is no good."

Her father squeezed her arms so tightly she thought he might break the skin. In an icy tone he said, "You will not marry James Reardon. You are going with us to Philadelphia."

Later when her mother found Jane sprawled on her bed convulsed with tears, her words were softer but showed no less resolve. "Dear child, James is a handsome charmer, but he is a lout. His reputation is not worthy of your affection." Sitting down on the bed beside her daughter and stroking the back of her head, Jane's mother continued, "Marriage is for a lifetime. Marriage is to establish a home, to nurture children, to love the Lord. The man who fathers your children must be trustworthy and good. Momentary passion must never rule your heart."

"But, Mother, I love him."

"Jane dear, in time you will know the meaning of love. It is far different from the infatuation you feel today. Believe me, this is for the best."

Jane was forbidden to see any more of James Reardon, but she was allowed to pen a brief note to be delivered by one of her brothers. She waited for his answer. She was certain James would come to their home and properly ask for and claim her hand. But James Reardon never appeared. He offered no protestation to her parents, made no effort to see her before their departure, and since her arrival in Philadelphia, no letter had come. Although mail was slow, it was reliable. Jane wondered if she would ever again feel that avalanche of tingles at the sight of another man. Or, if she could ever really trust another man.

One evening in late August as Jane and Jay walked back to her house, she took deliberate aim at a large rock in the center of the path and kicked hard. She stumbled, but when Jay reached to take her arm, she pulled away and ran.

"Jane, Jane, stop. What's the matter?

"Leave me alone. Just leave me alone," she sobbed, stopping to rub her foot.

Jay was baffled. An easy conversation had turned into a row, and he was at a loss as to what he had said or done. "Jane, did I say something? What's the matter?"

"No, nothing. You would never understand. Just leave me alone." Turning her back on him, she started to limp away.

Bewildered, Jay watched her retreating figure and then something deep inside his soul exploded. Anger. Fear. Love. This was not right. He wanted this woman and he had to know what was happening. In three long strides, Jay was beside Jane. He whirled her around and pressed his lips to hers. "Jane, Jane, please tell me what is the matter."

Her first impulse was to resist, push him away, until she felt that avalanche of tingles through her whole being and realized that this quiet, hardworking, trustworthy young man with whom she was building a rich and growing companionship was more than a good friend.

Much later that night, when Jane returned home, she tiptoed up the stairs, quietly entered her room, and sat down on the edge of her bed. For the first time since her arrival in Pennsylvania she was excited about her new life in this new land. She was excited about Jay Evans. She shook her head hard and laughed out loud as she realized all desire for

James Reardon had slipped beneath the horizon into the void of a forgotten past. Her mother had been right.

When Jay asked Jane to marry, she said yes.

It had taken three months for Jay to claim Jane's heart; it took almost four months for the Friend's Clearance Committee to investigate and the Society's women to declare them both worthy of the union. Jay and Jane received the Society's blessings in mid-November and the wedding date was set for the First Day of the First Month of the new year. In early December, Jay handed Jane a folded note from his mother inviting her for afternoon tea the following week.

The tall Case clock chimed as Lydia took Jane's heavy crimson cape and led her into the front parlor. Although Jane had been in the room numerous times over the past months, she still savored stepping onto the deep pile of the multi-colored Turkish carpet. A silver tea service with two porcelain cups and a plate of shortbread waited on the small round-top tea table that was polished to a soft luster and reflected the afternoon glow. After the two women were settled on the high-back settee covered in yellow damask, Lydia poured the tea and said, "Jane dear, I hope you're not chilled from your ride through the snow. The cold gives your cheeks such a delightful high color, almost the color of your cape."

"Thank you, Mother Lydia. The sun is bright so the ride was most invigorating, but your warm fire is certainly welcome."

The two women chatted about the weather for a few minutes until Lydia placed her cup on the table, faced her visitor directly, and said, "Jane dear, we are truly blessed that you are to wed our young Jay. He could not have found a more beautiful and grace-filled bride." Lydia's face, lined with the wrinkles of age, reflected joy as she spoke. "I asked you here today so we could have some time alone to get to know one another better...and I have something for you."

"Mother Lydia, it is I who am blessed to have won the heart of so fine a man. I am honored to be chosen as one of your family." Jane reached out to touch the small, thin, but still firm hand of the woman by her side. "Jay has shared your story. You are an incredibly brave woman."

"Hush now. It is all in a life. Our Lord is good," Lydia said. At fifty-seven, her hair was almost completely grey, but she still wore it long, pulled back in a neat bun, covered today with a simple but elegant house bonnet of French voile. Reaching into the side pocket of her green silk apron, her fingers caught the strings of the small leather pouch.

"Jane, I have something for you. Years ago, before we sailed for America, my husband, John, gave me a gift. It has come to symbolize my love for my husband...my love for my family...and my love of our Lord. At the time he purchased it, John was told an ancient fable about its power." Lydia paused to clear her throat before continuing. "It is said that she who wears the topaz absorbs God's light...she knows and acts on God's pre-planned destiny. I have always hoped that some day one of my daughters..." Lydia paused, unable to finish her sentence. "I want to pass along the charm." Placing the brilliant gem in her future daughter-in-law's hand, she said, "Jane dear, I want you to have the topaz."

Jane was speechless. She held the brooch up to the window filled with the bright afternoon light; the topaz cast beams in all directions. Jay had told her the story of his mother's topaz. She knew how much it meant to Lydia. The brooch would have been Rebecca's, had Rebecca lived. Awe and gratitude filled Jane's heart, mingled with a tinge of terror—the expectations. The responsibility.

"Oh Mother Lydia, it is lovely. How can I ever thank you? I shall wear it on our wedding day…and treasure it always."

CHAPTER SEVENTEEN

January 1st 1722

T he crisp, cold air was filled with anticipation on the
First Day in the First Month of the new year as the
congregation filed into the Meeting House. They knew
that this was the day that young John Evans, whom everyone called Jay, and Jane Howell would say their vows. Jane,
sitting on a side bench toward the front of the crowded hall,
wore a simple, full-skirted gown of emerald green brocade
with a low-cut bodice. A lacy white whisk, fastened at the
neck with the topaz brooch, modestly covered her neck and
shoulders. A small hood made of the same fabric as her dress
covered her luxuriant dark locks. Beside her sat her mother,
her father, and her two brothers. On the other side of the
hall on benches opposite to the Howells sat twenty-two-year-
old Jay, his mother, his father, his Aunt Mary, his Uncle
Tom, and his eight cousins, plus the spouses and children of
those cousins who were married. The Evans family filled the

first four rows on their side of the hall.

As was the custom at the beginning of a Quaker Meeting, the congregation sat in silent worship until someone felt moved to speak. On this morning, everyone waited in quiet contemplation and prayer until Jay lifted his head to catch Jane's eyes, the same emerald green as her gown, watching him. He gave a slight nod and he and Jane stood, walked to face each other in the center of the hall, and joined hands. Looking at this lovely woman before him, Jay said in a deep, modulated voice, "In the presence of God and these our Friends, I, John Evans, take thee, Jane Howell, to be my wife and promise, with divine assistance, to be a faithful and loving husband to care and provide for thee for as long as we may live."

Jane's smile was radiant as she looked into his hazel eyes and she responded in a clear, distinct tone, "In the presence of God and these our Friends, I, Jane, take thee, John, to be my husband and promise, with divine assistance, to be a faithful and loving wife to thee for as long as we may live."

David Lloyd, who was seated on the facing bench at the front of the hall, rose to read the certificate of their marriage that was to be signed by all the Friends who were present as witnesses to the wedding. After the ceremony the entire congregation was invited to the wedding feast at the Evans' foursquare stone house. It was a gala affair. In addition to the meats and mulled fruits the two mothers had prepared, Jane's father brought an amazing variety of special cakes and spiced sweets, and John, the proud father of the groom, served a special vintage of imported Madeira wine.

Throughout the afternoon, Jay, brimming with happiness, watched his vibrant new wife chat with their guests and tease the young children who clamored up and down the stairs and under the polished mahogany dining table.

Yet, one conversation out of earshot of the bride and groom was not fused with gaiety. John, David Lloyd, and two other of the elder Friends stood apart in a corner of the front parlor.

John was saying, "We invited her, she's like a member of the family. She sent Jane and Jay a beautiful weaving, came by the other day to give her blessings, but she said she best not come to the wedding."

David Lloyd nodding his head observed, "Her people's friendship has been abused. It is obvious they no longer trust any Englishmen."

"Lydia begged Leke Natap, but she said that her people would not stand for her being with us," John added.

"Can't blame them," one of the elders retorted, "Brother Penn's children, now that he is gone, no longer honor the treaty their father made. Penn's son continues to push the Lenne Lenape farther and farther north, claiming more and more of their land...this may mean trouble."

The other elder in the group shook his head slowly and said, "But these are our friends. It has always been said that the dress of a Quaker was better protection amongst the Indians than a musket."

"I'm afraid it may no longer be true." Lloyd responded, "It's rumored that with the latest betrayal the Lenne Lenape are talking with the Iroquois and other tribes to organize against all English settlements."

At that moment, Lydia's voice broke in from across the room. "John, Brother David, everyone come along, the bride and groom are leaving."

Climbing into the buggy parked in front of Jay's parents' house, the young couple, surrounded by well-wishers and loaded down with wedding gifts, were ready to head for their new home. In addition to fifty acres of fertile farmland along the river, John and Lydia had given Jay and Jane the clapboard cottage close to the mill.

Jane loved their small, two-room cottage overlooking the river. In early spring she spent much of her time outside planting and tending her new kitchen garden. Although Jay was gone working in the fields all day, every day except First Day, she never felt lonely; the continual motion and muted slosh of the mill's water wheel were pleasant company. And too, by mid-May she had four or five visits a week from neighboring farmers who brought their winter wheat to the Evans' mill for grinding into flour. Not only did Jane enjoy the neighbors' news and gossip, she liked weighing the raw grain and reckoning what the farmers would pay for the use of the giant grinding stones. She was good with numbers and liked the responsibility in the business affairs of the family.

On a particularly warm day in late June, the mid-morning summer sun was uncomfortably hot on her back and she wanted a break. Having weeded and tied up two rows of beans, she was heading for the well when she saw a lone figure coming through the woods toward the cottage. The stranger looked tired and a little lost, so Jane waved and shouted, "Good morning. Would you like a dipper of water?"

The stranger shuffled toward her, but when she caught a stench of stale whiskey and saw grime, Jane regretted her invitation. But it was too late. Although the day was hot, the stranger wore a filthy overcoat that hung in tatters on his huge frame and a large beaver hat pulled down over his ears. A straggly beard covered most of his face, and when he opened his mouth to speak, Jane saw huge gaps among the few remaining stumps of rotted teeth.

In a guttural growl, more animal than human, he said, "Yeah, I take water and eats," as he grabbed for her wrist.

Jane lunged to one side, barely avoiding his grasp and ran for the cottage. He, surprisingly quick on his feet, took two strides and caught hold of her skirt to stop her flight.

"Hey, little wench, not so fast."

Jane, half turning toward him, gave a furious kick. She heard the loud crack of her garden boot against his shin-bone; he winced, let out a loud shrieking "Damn!" but held tight to her skirt. She kicked again, hard, and grabbed at his chin whiskers, screaming like a banshee, "Let me go. Let me go." But he caught both of her wrists in one of his giant hands and with slow, menacing pressure pushed her down to her knees.

"Huh, a real wildcat needs some taming." With that, the stranger pulled a leather thong from around his waist and wrapped it tight around Jane's wrists. "Now, git up."

Jane remained on her knees, refusing to move or to look

up. Her hair had fallen loose and partially hid her face. She sat back on her heels making herself as compact as she could. She heard her blood pounding in her ears—an incessant beat in frantic rhythm like hoof beats pounding inside her head. Shaking her head violently she felt herself being dragged through the dirt and struggled beneath the vagrant's grasp. *Oh, could it be .... It was hoof beats.* Forcing all her weight in to her heels, Jane screamed as loud as she could.

"Git up, I say. Where's your man keep his money box?" The stranger yanked her up by a handful of her long hair.

Jane screamed loudly, "Help. Help!"

"Shut up and git moving," the stranger snarled, pushing her toward the house.

Jane knew she must stay outside. If anyone came on the road they would see her. As the stranger gave her a harsh shove, she sat down abruptly and screamed again, "Help. Help." It felt like every hair in her head was being yanked from her scalp. The stranger clamped his huge, filthy hand over her mouth. Opening her jaws as far as she could, Jane bit into his little finger. She felt skin burst and tasted blood, but then she felt a blow to the side of her head and everything went black.

Looking up into the familiar face of Josh Farmer, Jane asked, "Brother Josh, what happened?"

"Sister Jane, thank the Lord you are awake. A middle-aged man dressed in a homespun linen smock and breeches was kneeling beside her. "What an amazing woman!"

"What do you mean?" Jane whispered. Her throat felt parched and she had a horrible taste in her mouth.

"A prisoner off of one of the king's ships heading for the cane fields of Barbados escaped. The prison ship had put into Philadelphia for supplies and he somehow got ashore. You, brave lady, waylaid him long enough for the guards, who were on his trail, to spot him."

"Mistress Evans, I'm so pleased to see you awake." A tall, red-coated lieutenant standing a few yards away walked over and bent down beside her. "We've sent for your husband and a medic. They'll be here shortly."

Jane, now fully awake, realized she was lying on a pallet with a firm pillow underneath her head and a cool, damp cloth on her cheek. She moved her jaw wondering if anything was broken and felt pain, but it was not unbearable. Sitting up, she asked, "Could I please have some water? I've a horrible taste in my mouth."

The lieutenant nodded to a young lad beside him who scurried to the well. As Josh Farmer stood, the lieutenant knelt down and said, "We'd been on the convict's trail all morning. We knew we were close but worried that he would get away through those thick woods. It was your screams that led to his capture."

"Jane, Jane, are you alright?" In his haste to reach his wife, Jay nearly toppled over the kneeling lieutenant.

The young officer pulled himself upright, straightened his jacket, and said, "We are most impressed with your wife's bravery, Mister Evans."

Jay, seeing Jane smile and realizing she was not badly hurt, quickly retorted, "And I am most thankful you arrived when you did, Lieutenant." The two men stood and shook hands as the young lad, who had been sent to the well, handed Jane a tumbler of water. Murmuring her thanks, she swished the first mouthful round and round in her sore mouth, checking with her tongue that there were no loose teeth before spitting it out. She then gulped down what remained in the tumbler, so soothing to her dry, parched throat. Looking up at the two men talking, Jane did a quick comparison. The young lieutenant was good-looking with a nice face and lean frame, but no match to the finely chiseled, yet rugged features and strong body of her Jay.

When Lydia arrived, Jane had been moved inside the cottage. Her daughter-in-law was sitting propped up on her bed and Jay hardly finished filling in the details of the morning before Lydia declared, "Jane dear, you must come stay with John and me for awhile. You and Jay can take his old bedroom."

Jane smiled up at this kind woman and slowly shook her head. "Oh, thank you, Mother Lydia. That is so kind. But I am really fine. I love it here." Noting Lydia's expression of disbelief she hastened to add, "I promise to be more careful. I was really quite stupid not checking the man out before inviting him for a drink."

Lydia, though deeply fearful for her young, headstrong daughter-in-law, was not one to argue. She preferred to come at a problem obliquely. So, looking around the room she said, "The way you have decorated your cottage is lovely. It has so much life. I can see why you don't want to leave… but Jay is worried…we all are worried…maybe for a week or two..." A slight breeze caught the calico curtains at the window, showing off a vibrant splash of bright purple and vermillion red. Lydia realized that Jane's decor reflected Jane's personality, her character. Lydia knew it was best to say no more right then.

"Mother Lydia, really I'm fine. I want to stay here." The two women sat in silence for several minutes, and as Lydia stood to go the kitchen to brew some tea, Jane reached out, took the older woman's hand, and pulled her back down. "Mother Lydia, I want to tell you something." She sat up straighter and looked directly into her mother-in-law's hazel eyes. "Your gift gave me courage...you know, when that horrible creature grabbed me, I saw red. I was terrified. I felt trapped. But then as he pulled me to my knees, the strangest thing happened...it was as if my whole insides were filled with a golden glow, a radiant light. It gave me the courage to resist. I knew even though he was hurting me, I was protected. Mother Lydia, you gave me the power of the topaz. Thank you."

CHAPTER EIGHTEEN

1723–1736

The bundle of years that followed tumbled on and over one another in happy and joy-filled confusion. Through the years when Lydia and Jane tried to recall particular times or events, their memories were all a jumble. Those days were packed full of birthings and babies, toddlers, chores, schooling, Society meetings and socials, cooking and cleaning, coughs, work, and play. Jane and Jay's first child, named little Mary, was born late in the year of 1723.

Very soon after baby Mary's birth, Jane again found herself pregnant and became increasingly tired, a bit resentful, and a little overwhelmed by her new role as mother, as well as wife. When baby Lydia, named after her grandmother, was born eleven months after little Mary, Jane no longer resisted but welcomed Mother Lydia's plea, "Our house is much too big for just the two of us...and we plan to leave it to you and Jay anyway. Please let us share the joy and labor of your children, our grandchildren. Helping raise a family is truly a privilege, never a burden."

Jane never regretted Jay's and her decision to move in with Jay's parents and, as if to fulfill Lydia's wish, two little boy babies followed their sisters into the world. Before the move she worried that she would be tied down by her in-laws' expectations; but, instead, if there were any strings, they seemed to pull her to develop her own character and creativity. A deep and loving bond developed between Jane and Lydia, between Jane and her father-in-law John.

September 1736

Lydia watched the two men below, framed in the open second-story window beside her bed. They were almost the same height; the one of slender body stood erect, the other, solid and stooped. Their strides matched, moved together in a slow, hesitant rhythm as they walked to the cariole standing at the foot of the path. A handsome sorrel attached to the small carriage munched contentedly on the patch of late clover at the bottom of the hitching post and took no notice of their approach. The older man, John, her husband, walked with bent head and sloping shoulders, his hands thrust deep into the pockets of his worsted wool trousers. The shoulders of the younger man were straight, level as a finely planed plank. His hand rested lightly on John's shoulder. Lydia knew they were discussing her condition.

It was almost two months now since she had felt well

enough to ride into town, attend Meeting, or receive visi-
tors.Her stomach had not tolerated any victuals for nearly
that long, save an occasional cup of broth or slice of dry
toast. She knew John was worried. Fifty-six years was a long
time. Silently verbalizing her thoughts, Lydia mused, *We are
like an old braided rope, frayed and deeply scarred along the course of
its length, but the individual strands of fiber are so pounded together
that separation is impossible. John and I are one. We will be together
always, even when I return to our Maker. Shan't be long. I am ready.*

"Gran-Lydia, Mother wants to know if you would like
a cup of tea, now that the doctor is gone." Twelve-year-old
Mary, Lydia's eldest granddaughter, stood beside her bed
and reached for Lydia's hand and gave it a gentle squeeze.
Turning again to the open window, Lydia saw the doctor
pick up the reigns and touch the broad brim of his hat, a
simple gesture of farewell. As she watched her husband turn
to walk back to the house, Lydia knew that there would be
little change in the routines of his life after she was gone.
Jane ran a tidy house; John would not be neglected. Lydia
turned back to her granddaughter. Mary, so aptly named,
was born to nurture in the manner known only of a loving
soul. Lydia had not heard her come into the room. Mary's
presence was often felt before it was heard. The child's
comely face, framed by two long pigtails of thick blond hair
almost as coarse but much curlier than a horse's mane, still
held a trace of baby fat, and there was high color in her
cheeks. Mary inherited the ruddy complexion of the Evans,
John's side of the family, but not their height or large frame.

Like Lydia and her sisters from the Cledwyn clan, Mary would do well to reach much beyond five feet when fully grown. Lydia saw that the resemblance was strong between little Mary and her sister Mali, who was thirteen years of age when all the Evans left Wales so many, many years ago. Where was Mali today? Even though correspondence in those early years was infrequent, she usually received news at least once or twice a year. But after Mother and Father Cledwyn were gone and Barryn, the youngest of the brood was lost at sea, news from Radnorshire was sparse, brought only when a new immigrant from those parts arrived in Chester.

Jane's voice interrupted Lydia's reverie, "Good, you are still awake. I know the doctor's visit was tiring. I brought you some hot tea and ginger tincture. He said it should sooth your system, perhaps increase your appetite."

"Thank you, Jane dear. I will try after awhile. Right now, I was hoping Mary would read to me a bit from the Good Book." Jane nodded as she reached behind Lydia's head to fluff the pillow with three light punches. "Of course, I do hope you drink the tea later. You need some nourishment."

CHAPTER NINETEEN

October 1738

The afternoon sun was low in the sky, and in the distance Jane saw the deep purple foliage of John's oak, now in its maturity towering above their house. Its color was more subdued than the bright red leaves of the maple guarding the Evans family's burial plot, where she now stood. Jay's father had planted the oak over fifty years before, long before Jay was born. Now she, Jane, was standing beside the fresh dirt covering Jay's grave. Her husband Jay was gone. Stunning grief left Jane blank. An angry pain poured through her soul but with such penetration that it seemed to stifle any outward signs. She stood erect and shed no tears. Jay was dead.

A month ago, her husband, the man whom she cherished more and more with every year of their sixteen years of marriage, had gone to look at some land—a promising investment in the western part of the colony. In his absence she and the children were persuaded to be inoculated with the newly developed vaccine being distributed at the Meeting House. When Jay returned home he promised to ride into the hospital in Philadelphia to get vaccinated as soon as he got the chance, but with fall harvest beginning and the demands at the mill, he put it off. Last week he came home with a high fever, covered with an angry red rash and festering blisters. He went to bed. He never got up.

A sharp wind rustled the leaves above as Jay's father, now in his late sixties, pronounced a simple and eloquent farewell to his son. Jane stood stoically with an arm around young Evans, a towhead lad of four, and stared at the mound of dirt at her feet. Her other children, fourteen-year-old Mary, twelve-year-old Lydia, and ten-year-old John, stood directly behind her, each wrapped in his or her own silent grief. At the conclusion of Jay's father's remarks, family and friends, one by one, solemnly approached the widow and the father of Jay Evans. Each in turn gave a gentle hug or quiet murmur of condolence.

As John stood acknowledging the gestures of these friends, his world was closing down. Today he had buried his only son. The smallpox scourge had taken a robust, god-fearing man in his prime; Jay was dead at thirty-eight. Ten feet away a small headstone marked the grave of the woman he would forever cherish above all else in the world. Lydia, his gentle, courageous Lydia, slipped away two years ago surrounded by family and close friends. On that fateful day, John, kneeling at her side with his ear held close to her lips, had heard her last words, "John, my love, joy is mine. I see a beautiful golden light."

John's eyes shifted to the stone marking the grave next to Lydia's—*Rebecca Evans, 1681–1695*. Through resigned forbearance and his deep love for his wife, he had eventually accepted Rebecca's loss but never truly forgiven himself for the death of his precious daughter. The memory of that beautiful little girl always drove piercing pain into the dormant but never-quite-healed wound at the center of his being. Beyond those two headstones he saw the graves of his father, John, his mother, Elizabeth, and his brother, Tom. Except for his sister, Liz, who had married and moved to New York years ago, all of the family who had journeyed with him from Wales was buried in this small plot of Pennsylvania soil. Evans' roots were well established in this new land.

Although devastated, John had not been left alone. He wondered if Lydia had somehow foretold the future, saw the coming of this day. Fifteen years before, shortly after the birth of Jay and Jane's first child Lydia insisted that the young family move into the large stone house with them. Those were raucous and joyous times, three new babies in six years, then a six-year hiatus until the last baby, Evans, was born. Over the years, John gradually and willingly acceded his position as household head to his son Jay. The example of his father, who lived with his brother, Tom, after they all came to Pennsylvania, had taught him well. Now with the death of his son, John was once again head of the household. With decreasing energy and a leaden heart, this bereaved man recognized his responsibility for

Jay's handsome widow and four young children. Yet, he knew it was not the burden that it might have been. Jane was a capable woman.

In the months following Jay's death, John resumed management of the farm and the mill that he gradually had turned over to Jay, but he wasted no time implementing his plan for the future. Over the years he had noted Jane's avid interest and good sense in the running of the family's business operations. She was an eager participant in all that John taught Jay about the management of their properties. John now realized that Jane had a much better business head than any of his brother's now adult male children and began priming her for the time when all of their holdings would belong to her and his four grandchildren. John also knew he needed to prepare Jane to ward off the grasp that would likely come from the male members of their extended family once he was gone and she was fully in charge.

John lived less that two years beyond the day that he buried his son. John died late in April of 1740. The farm, the mill, the house, and the children were now the sole responsibility of his daughter-in-law, Jane Howell Evans. John Evans had bequeathed his estate and all of his worldly goods to Jane for her lifetime, to be passed on to his grandchildren upon her death.

June 1740

"Cousin Benjamin, what brings you here on this warm afternoon?" The clover was thick underfoot as Jane came up from the near pasture with her two sons. She was tired but satisfied, having walked the three lower pastures with the boys and Clarence, the new hired-hand who was learning the ropes from Rufus. The stone walls were in good repair. She stepped to the garden gate as Jay's cousin Benjamin, a portly man in his mid-fifties, fastidious in dress, dismounted from his dapple-grey gelding. With slow, deliberate movements, he took a large, linen handkerchief from his trouser pocket, lifted his broad-rimmed hat, and wiped the perspiration from his brow, saying, "Sister Jane, I have been wanting to have a conversation with you since Uncle John's funeral. May we go inside?"

"Why of course. Boys, give your greetings to Brother Benjamin and then finish feeding the pigs. Lemonade and sweets are yours when your chores are done." She smiled at her sons, proud of the way they had stepped in to try to fill first their father's and then their grandfather's shoes.

"Those lads are sprouting like beanstalks. You must be feeding them well," observed Benjamin.

"I have been blessed with four fine children. Mary and Lydia also flourish. My children are a great comfort and tremendous help in managing our place."

As Benjamin followed her up the steps onto the back porch, Jane called to Mary, who appeared in the kitchen door and asked, "Mary, will you please squeeze up some lemons and bring lemonade and sweets to the parlor?"

On entering the parlor, Jane pointed to a cane-bottom chair saying, "Brother Benjamin, it is so warm this afternoon, that chair free of fabric will likely be a cooler seat." Removing his hat and settling into the large, simply styled chair, Benjamin said, "Jane, I prefer that our conversation be in private, just the two of us."

At these words, Jane sensed a warning irritation under her heart but kept her voice light, "Why of course, Brother Benjamin. Mary will not be long with our drinks and then we can be left alone." She sat down on a small side chair on the opposite side of the room and asked, "How is your family? I see them on First Day Meetings but recently have not had opportunity to inquire as to their health."

Benjamin gave a perfunctory report on each of his seven children's health and activities and lapsed into uncomfortable silence. Jane, not inclined to relieve the silence, sat looking out the window at her sons herding the cows to the barn for their evening milking. She had heard rumors that the men in the Society were "concerned for her welfare." Last week, Susan Smith repeated in confidence the conversation she overheard between her husband and others after Meeting. "No woman is capable of managing a farm...what is more, a mill...such affairs were the business of men...something has to be done." Jane surmised that Brother Benjamin, a well-respected officer of the Welsh Tract's Men's Meetings and elected member of the Pennsylvania Assembly, as well as her father-in-law's nephew, was the agreed-upon agent.

Mary, a robust sixteen-year-old with a freckled face and a full head of straw blonde curls sprouting out from under her small house bonnet, appeared carrying a large tray with six glass tumblers, a pitcher of lemonade, and a plate of sweets. As she entered the room she turned to Benjamin and said,

"Brother Benjamin, it is surely a delight to see you looking so well." The children, accustomed to helping their mother entertain visitors, were well schooled in company manners.

Jane said, "Ah, Mary, this looks lovely. Thank you. Do set the tray down, it is heavy." Mary placed the tray on the round-top tea table, and Jane poured two tumblers of lemonade, asking her daughter to hand one to Brother Benjamin. "Now, dear, Brother Benjamin says he wants a conversation in private with me, so will you pass him some sweets and take the tray? You children may have your lemonade in the garden. The boys will be pleased not to have to clean up before refreshment."

Mary gave her mother a quizzical look but said, "Yes, Mum," and retreated out of the room with the tray.

Benjamin took a long swallow from the glass and nibbled at a ginger wafer before he spoke. "Sister Jane, you are a remarkable woman. It shows in your children."

"Thank you, Brother Benjamin. I am blessed," Jane said. Sitting erect, she fingered the hem of her green apron and watched closely as the man across the room gathered his words.

"At the men's council last week, your problem was discussed."

"What problem is that?" Jane inquired in a low, even tone. "I know of no problem."

"Ah, Sister Jane, though Uncle John's will granted you a life estate in his property, you are without a man to manage your affairs. That must weigh heavily on your soul. The men of our Society want to do right by you. I am here to offer my assistance."

Jane chose her next words carefully. She must not give offense, but she must not give in. Jay's father had warned her that the men in the Society would try to take over the management of her affairs. That was customary, but, in spite of custom, he said that he believed she was best able to manage his properties. Wanting to ensure his grandchildren's inheritance and determined to protect his judgment, he had gone to an outsider, an independent counsel—not a Friend—to write his last will and testament.

"Brother Benjamin, I am honored by your concern, but in truth I feel no need of such assistance. Jay and I worked closely together in all things…after he was gone, though his father monitored our affairs, it was I who managed our properties from day to day." Her heart raced, she wanted to yell for this officious man to get out of her house, but she held her temper and took a long, deep breath. "Please know that all is in good order."

Benjamin Evans watched Jane's cheeks flame a deep red. This was going to be difficult. Jay's widow, like a high-spirited colt, needed to be treated with a firm but gentle hand. Brother Benjamin was known as an effective, skilled negotiator in the colonial legislature—rigid but fair.

"We in the Society always honor the equal partnership between a man and wife within their marital bond. Our concern in no way questions your abilities as the spiritual leader of your household. The deportment of your children gives more than adequate testimony in that area. However, such responsibility certainly occupies you fully. Now with

Uncle John gone, it is for the management of his businesses that I offer my experience and assistance…to relieve you of that burden."

In as even a tone as she could manage, Jane responded, "But Brother Benjamin, according to your uncle's will, his businesses is now my business."

"Why yes, in the strict letter of the document, but for the welfare of the children, for your own good, we in the Society deem it best that some type of overseer, a guardian or trustee, be charged with advising you in your financial affairs. It was thoroughly discussed at last Thursday's Meeting and I was asked to take on that responsibility, which I willingly accepted."

Jane stood, took a deep breath, and squared her shoulders; her father-in-law's words rang in her ears: *Jane, I am leaving the management of my properties to you. Over the years I have observed that your head for business is much better than most of the men in our family. My will stipulates my wishes. You must protect my grandchildren's interests.* She said, "Brother Benjamin, I appreciate your concern, but Father John's will clearly states that I inherit and am to manage his property during my lifetime. If you have any doubt, please call on Joseph Freeman, the lawyer who prepared the will. He can clarify the matter."

"Joseph Freeman? Is he not the Scottish Presbyterian who arrived from Aberdeen last year? How strange that Uncle John went to a lawyer outside the Society for the creation of his will."

Jane said nothing.

Over the next few years, Jane and her children attended First Day Meeting every week and in addition to regular school attendance at the Friends school next to the Meetinghouse, the children enjoyed the frequent gatherings and outings of the Quaker young folk. Jane, honoring the family tradition, wanted Jay's children to grow up in their father's as well as her faith. Friends were cordial and polite, yet Jane wondered. Was there an undercurrent of reserve, a lack of complete acceptance within the Society? No longer was she given responsibilities at Women's Meeting, whereas in previous years there were times when she had felt overburdened with leadership tasks. Nor was she anylonger asked to serve on a Clearance Committee to investigate the worthiness of a potential bride or groom. Jane was not particularly concerned. That was their business. Her energies were well occupied with running the farm, making the mill profitable, and seeing to it that her children were well educated and had a good life.

Yet, one thing bothered her. Mary was twenty years old, not a beauty, but a most attractive young woman with a generous heart bursting with enthusiasm. Over the last two years, several young men in the Society had come calling, all smiles and solicitous overtures. But after several months, each, in turn, did not come back. Were they being warned that Mary was a woman who would not find favor with the Clearance Committee? Had she, Jane, poisoned her daughter's marriage possibilities? To go outside the Society for matrimony was unthinkable. That would create a total break for a Quaker, and the Society was Mary's life.

One morning while she and Mary were still in the kitchen

after the other children had gone to school, Jane said, "William Adams has not come calling in several weeks. Did you two have an argument?"

"Oh, no," answered Mary in a cheerful voice. "He seems quite smitten with Lucy Waters. I do think they make a handsome couple, don't you?"

Jane looked at her daughter. Her response seemed sincere. Mary's life increasingly revolved around her activities at the new orphanage in town. Her sunny disposition and loving attention was certainly a godsend to abandoned and lonely children. Was this to be her daughter's life? Cherishing other people's children? She longed to talk over this dilemma with Jay. But Jay was gone.

September 1746

On a First Day late in September, nearly eight years after Jay's death, Jane filed out of the Meetinghouse behind a group of chatting women and felt a tap on her shoulder. When she turned, she was surprised to be facing the widower Jordan Smith, a farmer from the next county, not a regular member of the congregation, but a man she had known casually for years. His first words, self assured and direct, told her that here was a man of action, a man who felt comfortable in the world. "Sister Jane, may I have permission to call on you next week sometime?"

Jordan Smith, about ten years older than she, farmed in New Castle. He did not often frequent the Chester Meeting, and now, with this query, Jane suspected that his recent attendance might be because of her. Jordan Smith was not unattractive. He was well built, had graying hair, was about her height, and well spoken. What was it that the bards say about the seven-year cycle? Was it closure time for her period of mourning? It felt good to have a man want to visit, even if it might merely be for business rather than social reasons, but she wanted to find out.

"Of course, how about next Wednesday afternoon?"

On Wednesday afternoon, Brother Jordan came to her house for a brief visit, and Jane invited him to return for dinner the following First Day. When that First Day came, twelve-year-old Evans was the only one of her children at home. Mary had persuaded her brother John to help her at the orphanage, and their sister Lydia had gone to a friend's house for the afternoon. Seeing his mother scurrying about setting the table, Evans asked, "Mother, why is Brother Smith coming to dinner? He's never been here before."

"Oh, Evans he was here Wednesday while you were over playing with Jacob." Reaching out to rumple his hair, Jane smiled at her son. Almost as tall as she, Evans was a pole of a boy, waiting for weight to catch up with last summer's growth spurt. Of all her children, Evans was the most protective; he assumed a proprietary air about all of her activities and associations. "He is a nice man. I met at Meeting. I think you will like him," Jane said.

"Is his wife coming?

"His wife died several years ago."

"Does he have any children?"

"His children are grown with families of their own."

Evans eyed her suspiciously and asked, "'How old is he?'"

"Well, I'm not really sure, probably in his mid-fifties. Now run wash up before he gets here."

Seeing Jordan Smith riding up the lane to the house, Jane scurried to the hall mirror to smooth back her hair. She gave a bemused grimace at the grey strands beginning to appear at her temples and straightened her house bonnet before opening the door. In a playful, near clowning manner, Jordan stepped inside, swept off his hat, gave a slight bow, and presented her with a large bouquet of blue heliotrope and Shasta daisies. Jane smiled broadly and laughed out loud at the way he filled the front hall with his good humor. When he winked at Evans standing by his mother's side, the young boy thought he could probably like this man—he was funny.

A place was set at the Evans' table for Jordan Smith every First Day throughout the winter. The family enjoyed his stories and silly jokes; his unassuming good nature fit easily into the rhythm of their lives. One afternoon in early spring at the conclusion of their First Day dinner, the young folks scattered and Jordan turned to Jane saying, "Could we go see the new foal Evans has been talking about?'

"Our mare and her new foal are in the pasture behind the barn. She's a beauty. I'd love for you to see her," Jane responded.

As they walked through the tender green grass, Jordan turned to Jane and said, "Sister Jane, I hope you know how very much I admire you. You have such a fine family. It is true joy to be with you. I never believed I would feel such happiness again."

Jane turned to look at him, noticing the sharp outline of his neatly trimmed beard and said, "Ah, Jordan, you are always welcome. We all enjoy your company so very much."

The two walked on in silence, drinking in the fresh spring air until Jordan stopped abruptly and reached for Jane's hand. "Jane. Jane, could you ever agree to become a true part of my life? I very much honor Brother Jay's memory, but I promise with all my heart I would make you a good husband."

For the last two months, Jane had sensed that she would have to face this question. On countless winter nights, through many sleepless hours, she had wrestled with her response. In only a few years, Mary and Lydia would most likely be married, John and Evans would also be adults, establishing their own families. She would be alone. Jordan Smith was a good man, respectable, comfortable, delightful company. She was attracted to him. She missed male companionship. To once again have the warmth of a man's arms would be good. But then...she grappled with conficting thoughts, ambivalent feelings, turning them over and over in her mind and heart.Wishing for clarity, she became increasingly confused, until finally two nights before, after wrestling with indecision for hours, she had slipped out of bed, shuffled with bare feet to the small bedroom hearth, and placed a spunk in the tinderbox to light a candle. Then, lifting the lid of the rosewood box atop her dresser, she had taken Lydia's topaz out of its pouch, held it to the flickering flame, and prayed long and hard for guidance. The answer had come.

Now leaving her hand in Jordan's hand she looked directly at him and with a gentle, solemn voice said, "Jordan, you are a wonderful man. I admire you greatly and am deeply honored by your feelings. But, you must know the truth. I will never re-marry."

Jane knew she was married to her land and to the heritage of her children.

CHAPTER TWENTY

On a backwoods trail in western Pennsylvania in the summer of 1758, a Delaware Indian (a Lenne Lenape) the colonists called Daniel, cursed both England and France. "Damn you!" he exclaimed to a British emissary, "why do not you and the French fight on the sea? You come here only to cheat the Indians and take their land from them.
—Early Western Travels, Reuben Gold Thwaites, ed.

October 1753

There were about twenty of them, men in red coats carrying muskets tramping in the lower pasture, foraging fodder for their mounts and anything edible for themselves. Jane had watched from the house but felt helpless—opposed to the whole business, this war that pitted the English, and thus the Pennsylvanians, against the Iroquois and the French. Through the trickery of Thomas Penn, who inherited his grandfather William's holdings, their trusting Lenne Lenape friends, the original people of these lands, had been driven out almost twenty years before. Why wouldn't the natives fight back? Why shouldn't they? But war, fighting, could never be the right way to resolve such differences.

Now, it was difficult to know who was fighting whom.

The loyalties of the natives were continually changing. But who could blame them, since the white man's word was too often unreliable? The Quakers, opposed to war, held the majority in the Pennsylvania Assembly and refused to send troops to join the fray or give financial support. Yet, her own son John, inflamed by the burning of a colonial settlement by French-allied Indians in northern Virginia, had renounced his Quaker heritage and joined an English regiment under Major George Washington marching to the Ohio River.

Though Jane opposed fighting on principle, she admitted to herself that these very men who were scrounging in her fields could be her salvation—the protectors of her land should the French direct the Iroquois to destroy it. Taking a large basket from the pantry shelf, she climbed down into the cool, damp cellar to the barrel of sweet, firm apples that she and Evans had gathered last month.

The young soldiers were obviously surprised at her approach. "Where are you fellows from?"

A corporal who could not be a year over nineteen, the obvious leader of the group, responded, "Virginia, Ma'am."

Setting the basket in their midst, she said, "I brought something for you to eat." Each in turn took several apples from the basket, respectfully expressing gratitude. These boys were obviously from good families. She hoped someone was offering her son John the same largess, wherever he might be...

July 1756

"Natap, is that really you? It has been so long. Come, come sit down." The middle-aged Indian woman, whom Jane had not seen in years, shuffled onto the porch and sighed into a cane rocker. Scabs and scratches covered her bare arms and her nails were broken and dirty. Streaks of soot marked the front of the simple brown dress that hung from her bent shoulders.

"Thank you, Jane. These are bad times." Natap paused and, with dark eyes cast down, massaged her temples in a slow, deliberate, circular motion. Jane watched but said nothing. Finally, clasping her fingers together and lowering her hands to her lap, Natap looked up at Jane. "My husband is dead, my sons gone. English raiders burnt our village. Our Lenne Lenape men who were left fled north to join the Iroquois and fight alongside the French." She looked intensely into Jane's face. "I had to come warn you."

"Sit here, Natap. Let me fetch you something to drink. You must be hungry. How far have you come?" As Jane went to the kitchen, Natap's fatigue settled into the contours of the chair. Rocking back and forth, she looked out over the green pasture but saw only the images of flame and fleeing souls that were etched on her inner eye. She was grateful her mother Leke Natap was no longer alive to witness such horror. *What does the white man want? Pushing, pushing, forever pushing us off the land. Fighting, killing. But this is not the way of the Evans. When I was a little girl, Sister Lydia taught me to read. Gave me a Bible. Said underneath it all we were all God's children. She said she wanted me to understand Jesus' message of peace. I never really understood it all but it harmonized with the teaching of the Great Spirit my people worship and the Evans were so kind. Even in their time of great sorrow. When my friend Rebecca died, I thought they might not want to see me, I would only remind them of their loss. But Mother insisted that I go often to sit with Sister Lydia, read to her. Sister Lydia was always kind, but so sad. Her sorrow was so great she had stopped reading to herself, said the words just swam around on the page. But when I read to her, she would close her eyes and seemed to absorb the meaning. Now Sister Lydia, her husband, Brother John, and their son, young Jay, are gone. All the Evans except Jane and her children are gone. But they carry the family's spirit. They are good people. I had to warn them.*

"Here, Natap, let us wipe your hands and face before you try to eat." Jane kneeled before the sitting woman, gently sponged the grime off her face with a damp cloth, and said, "Now sit still, we don't want to get your clothes wet." She placed a bowl of warm water in Natap's lap and, with great care, guided Natap's roughened fingers into the water, gingerly rubbing the woman's hands and arms over with soap. After rinsing off the soap, she removed the bowl and patted Natap's arms and hands dry. Jane then laid a piece of molding bread that she kept for such emergencies on Natap's left arm across a deep cut. Years ago when a mule kicked Jay, Dr. Graven had taught her that mold would keep a wound from festering. Natap must have possessed the same knowledge for she gave Jane a knowing nod.

"Now do you think you can eat a bit? Eat and rest. We

will talk later." With her injured arm resting by her side, Natap managed with her right hand to spoon up the barley soup Jane held before her.

"Thank you, Jane. I was hungry." She placed the spoon in the empty bowl and pushed away Jane's hand. "Now, I must tell why I am here. My people, the Shawnees, the Mingos, and the Cayugas have joined with the Iroquois and are seeking revenge. We can no longer trust the English who make false promises and continue to push us off our land. The warriors are headed this way. I'm not sure when they will get here, but when they do come, my sons will be with them. My sons grew up on stories of the good Evans. We always referred to your family as our white family. My sons know about you. They never tired of their grandmother's tales about your goodness. If they see me here, I believe, I hope, my sons can convince the others in the war party to pass you by. There is much anger in the hearts of the Lenne Lenapes and the others."

Jane swallowed hard, seeking to mask the fear that made her stomach spasm. Thank goodness young John was in Ohio with Colonel Washington. He would jump to do battle at the first sight of approaching Indians. Evans and the girls would listen. They would heed her advice. Yet, Natap's influence, her pleas, might not be enough.

"How much time do you reckon before they get here?" Jane asked. She must prepare the children. Explain all this to them. The girls working in Philadelphia, Lydia as a nurse's aide and Mary at the orphanage, would be home by late afternoon, and Evans would be coming in from the fields shortly.

"I don't think they will get here for a couple of days. I had a good head start and tried to keep moving through the night. They will make camp, take longer rests when darkness falls."

"Come Natap, you must rest now."

"Thank you, Jane. You are right, I am very tired."

"Well, if you don't come inside this moment, stretch out on a proper bed, I fear you will be asleep in that chair before we can get you there."

The warring French and Indian tribes never reached the Evans' property. A backwoods scout warned a unit of British soldiers stationed south of Chester of the French and Indian movements. The soldiers quickly responded and mounted a fierce battle twenty miles west of New Castle, driving back the advancing warriors. When Natap returned to her people, she was told that both of her sons had been killed.

CHAPTER TWENTY-ONE

October 1792

"**M**istress Jane, Mistress Jane, see what I brung you." Jane woke with a start and looked at the barefoot carrot-top standing before her, gap-toothed and smiling, holding out a red apple in grubby hands. It took a minute for her to come to her senses and focus her eyes. She looked up into the heavy branches of John's oak, now over a century old, with width and breadth to match its years. She had fallen asleep in the warm afternoon sun on their back porch, a half-finished sweater and knitting needles lay in her lap. She knew that the small boy standing before her belonged to the new couple who had arrived to help Evans with the harvest, but what was his name? "Why, thank you, sonny. Have you been helping your parents?" she asked, taking the apple. Feeling the firm flesh of the fruit, she brought it to her nose to inhale its sweet scent.

"Yes, Ma'am. Mama and them are still in the orchard.

She told me to bring you the biggest apple I could find."
Jane shook her head and looked at the young lad before her.
"Tell me your name again."

"Jamie McFarland," responded the boy. "What're you knitting?"

"Why, this is a sweater for one of the children at the orphanage in the city, my daughter's orphanage."

Even though their land had know relative peace for the last eight years, the number of babies and young children left without family since the war, was legion. Jane, ninety years old and unable to do much around the farm, was thankful that she could contribute in her small way, to help Mary with "her" children.

Jane's thoughts drifted. Jay had been dead more than fifty years. Fifty years, why, that was greater than a lifetime for most people. She marveled that she had lived so long; she marveled at the monumental events she had witnessed and the astounding differences in the lives and opportunities of the Evans family since that fateful night when Mother Lydia crept down into the dark Welsh dungeon to exchange clothes with Jay's father.

Jane had dedicated her life to assuring the accomplishment of the family's dream—the preserving of their Pennsylvania lands for their descendents, the four grandchildren of that brave Welsh couple. She reached up to touch the brooch pinned to the chambray scarf at her neck and fingered the gem's smooth surface. For a reason Jane could not comprehend, she felt a surge of strength coarse through her stiff limbs and caught a vision of Lydia, Jay's diminutive mother, smiling at her.

As the vision faded, Jane's mind turned to the sober realization that the dedicated commitment that carried two generation of Evans through years of hardship, as well as periods of prosperity, now hung on a slender thread. Her grandson, young Sam, was their last hope. Two of Jay's and her children, Lydia and John's grandchildren, had moved far away. Only three of their direct descendents still lived in Pennsylvania—Mary, with an abundance of children at the orphanage but with no husband and children of her own, Evans, and Samuel, Evans' adult son, whose mother had died in childbirth. Those three were the last of the line living on the Evans' land.

How different her life had been from what she had imagined when Lydia first presented her with the brooch on that December day so very long ago. Yet, in some strange way, Jane knew that the light, the tenacious bravery the topaz represented, had seen her through so many years of turbulence and uncertainty—two wars and the creation of an independent nation. It had been hard, but she had managed somehow to hold on until her son Evans returned from fighting and was ready to take over the family properties.

As Jane sat rocking, watching the play of shadows on the ground under the oak, she mused that the real difficulties seem to have escalated in the late 1760s, shortly after the war with the French and the Indians was settled. Second and third generation colonials were beginning to chafe under British rule. She thought back on the frequent gatherings of irate neighbors that met in the Evans' parlor in those times. At first she had been startled to see the many different types of people who came to their house. They were such a varied lot—different backgrounds, different religions, different occupations, different social standings. Yet, as she listened to the explosions of words filling their parlor—individuals voicing deep concern over the right to shape their own destiny—she realized that the common cause among these patriots made the differences between them of no consequence. Their freedom as individual citizens was at stake. These people—farmers, artisans, laborers, merchants, trappers, bankers, shippers— were all threatened by the draconian restrictions on trade the British Parliament was enacting in faraway London. The ever-increasing taxes imposed by British rulers were strangling their livelihood. It was taxation without representation. Their civil liberties as English citizens were being abused. It was at one of those gatherings that Jane learned that Jeremiah Streete, a Friend and her commercial agent, had been thrown in prison, charged with evading a newly established export duty, and tried without due process by a hastily formed Court of Admiralty rather than by the proper, legally established colonial court.

When the first shots between the British redcoats and the colonial American Minutemen were fired at Lexington and Concord in 1775, her son Evans followed his brother John's decision to renounce his Quaker pacifism. Both John and Evans joined the army of the rebellion; young Sam, her grandson then a teenager, stayed home to help her with the farm for about a year, but then he too left to join General Washington and the fight for independence from unbearable British strictures.

Thankfully, both of her sons, John and Evans, and her grandson, Sam. survived the war years, but when the fighting was over and they returned home, John left their homestead in Pennsylvania to carve out new holdings in the Valley of the Ohio. Jane had not heard from him in years. Evans and Sam remained with her on their land to tend to their properties; Evans also wanted to help establish their new nation's government. She had wondered if he would remarry, but business and politics, plus trying to hold on to the farm and mill during those turbulent years of war and its aftermath, had seemed to consume all of his interest and energy.

Jane watched the young lad who, having delivered his apple, run back across the field to his family in the orchard. She thought of her great grandchildren in England, children she would never know, wondering if they felt so free as young Jamie McFarland. It was over forty years since her daughter Lydia, affectionately called Little Lydia, had sailed for England. In the late 1750's, during the French and Indian War, Little Lydia had served as a nurses' aide in the hospital in Philadelphia where she met Geoffrey Land, a British army captain from Surrey. A troop of redcoats had been quartered outside the city and Geoffrey had come to inspect the wounded. From that day on, Lydia and Geoffrey spent all of their free time together, and before Geoffrey returned to England, Little Lydia renounced her family's faith, married Geoffrey in the Anglican Church of Philadelphia, and sailed with him to his homeland.

Picking up her knitting to see if she had dropped any stitches, Jane smiled to herself at one of life's strange ironies— her daughter Lydia Evans, the namesake of that brave Welsh woman Lydia Evans, had crossed the Atlantic ocean to start a new life just as her grandmother had done seventy years earlier—yet, Little Lydia had gone in the opposite direction.

When the Revolutionary War broke out, Jane had worried that her sons would meet her son-in-law in battle, but thankfully, Geoffrey had resigned his commission and was no longer serving in the regular army. Her son-in-law and his family never returned to American soil. Jane received an occasional letter from her daughter in England and knew that little Lydia and Geoffrey's two sons both had children of their own about the age of young Jamie McFarland.

"Mother, it is growing dark. Come in, you must not take a chill." Jane had not noticed Evans come out on the porch but was glad for the support of his arm as they stepped inside. When she sat too long her joints became unbearably stiff.

As they ate pea soup and flatbread prepared earlier by the young neighbor girl Evans hired to watch after the house and his mother while he was away during the day, Evans said, "Remember my telling you about Alexander Lowry, the Indian trader from Western Pennsylvania who served under General Washington during the war and was later a Congressional delegate from that area?"

"Why yes, I think you brought him to the house several

times. From Ireland isn't he?"

"Yes, from the northern part around Donegal, Derry, I think. But he's lived in Western Pennsylvania for years. Lowry's young daughter by his second wife came to Philadelphia with him on this trip, and your grandson, who met her last week, seems quite smitten. Sam wants to bring them out to dinner on Sunday."

"Oh. It would be nice to see Mr. Lowry again. How old is his daughter?"

"I don't think she is yet twenty, but a handsome lass that would easily turn any man's head. Frances is her name. Frances Lowry."

"Well, I hope there is a mutual attraction. It is certainly time for our young Sam to start his family," Jane said, as she fingered the face of the smooth brooch at her neck, wondering, *Could this be the lass destined to wear the topaz?*

CPSIA information can be obtained at www.ICGtesting.com
Printed in the USA
LVOW130354010413

326825LV00003B/7/P